THE LAST DAYS OF THE WAKE MEN

The Martians Invade the Victorian Fenland

C.A. Powell

CONTENTS

INTRODUCTION

(THE MARTIAN'S PREDICAMENT)

The Martian was alive! It looked around within the damaged capsule and was confused. It wondered how such a thing could happen. The insidious bipeds of this strange world seemed to be adapting. They were bringing down Martian fighting machines – the protective armour of the invasion force. How could this be?

One, maybe more, of the mechanical legs of the stricken machine had been destroyed. Now, water sprayed inside the machine's ruptures – the whole trunk had smashed into the lake. The creature recalled the shimmering liquid coming up to meet the viewer screen as the huge mechanism gave way and the control cabin toppled forward.

There had been explosions under the water. Each time, around the contraption's legs. The bipeds of the strange new world had organised such a thing. They had executed it with precision. Again, how could this be?

An associate pilot companion had already evacuated via the emergency exit. The crew member had not waited to check its other companion. The now solitary and abandoned Martian creature understood and would have done the same, but it spared a thought. Something was going wrong with the invasion. The herding of lesser creatures was not working with the bipeds. They were different from the way of lesser creatures on Earth and the Martian home world. These bipeds seemed to be resisting and hiding. They retreated but still tried to fight. Now and then, they killed Martians. They were more dangerous than expected. Earth was full of unexpected things. Now the alien creature had witnessed what the devious bipeds could do. They had a rudimentary technology and, though primitive, sometimes it could be formidable. Much had been underestimated.

The creature's feeler moved across the controls and tried to pull the cylinder from the panel clasps. The apparatus was ruptured and useless. The small heat ray device could not work if the cylinder was split. The notion of any form of armament was dismissed. The alien realised it would need to abandon vessel with no weapon – the companion had taken the other.

The creature's thick lower abdominal standing feelers lifted its sick and perspiring bulk. Three thick support coils slithered its form towards the open emergency hatch, a giant sluggish being with multiple arm-like tendrils, leaving its artificial protective cocoon. The alien's thin upper appendages with three little twisting digits clasped the side of the hatch opening and pulled its entire bulk out of the wrecked machine.

The cold breeze of the night was unnerving. There was sporadic noise – biped noise! Somewhere in the black smoke, the Martian could hear the calls of the approaching creatures of this strange world. The crackle and bang of their strange fire sticks. The diabolical bipedal creatures that fought back. The ones that wore contraptions over their hideous faces, vile artificial faces that allowed them to fight inside the poison gas. The bipeds were adaptable and quick to learn. How did they make themselves new faces? How had they become more dangerous?

The creature rasped painfully through its curved beak and coughed out some blood. The Martian knew it was ill and clearly suffering from something. Perhaps, various things. The wretched being had also been injured by the fall of the machine, but it did not matter. The off-world body was ailing before the biped attack – the companion had been unwell too. Other fighting machine crews were afflicted and there was speculation of poisoned food. There was never poison on the home world. Why was this new world so different?

Amid the commotion of unseen bipeds and their shouting noises, the creature allowed its injured form to slide down the curve of the machine. It plunged into the water and used its tendrils to pull and paddle its form away from the stricken and destroyed fighting machine.

The commotion grew louder, and the partially submerged alien peered through the mist towards the cacophony of noise, its huge beak below the waterline, but its big bulbous eyes above. Then came the fizzing sound of a small feeler-held phaser. The escaped crew companion had fired at a biped somewhere in the mist. The scream of the biped target could be clearly heard. But then followed the cascade of bangs and fire flashes in wicked reply – the strange biped weapons that slung projectiles at speed. The same little metal missiles that were often heard bouncing off the fighting machine's armour. The projectiles would smash straight through an exposed Martian hide and explode out of the other side, tissue and innards spraying everywhere. The bipeds were formidable in face-to-face confrontation.

Amid the flashes of light and biped shooting sounds came the scream of the companion. A

Martian call of pain, and the assumption that the crew member was hit by a small biped missile. The agony of such a strike could only be imagined. What more wicked things were these vicious bipeds capable of?

Next came the sequence of water displacement as the companion's form slithered into view completely panic-stricken. The hunter had become the hunted. The associate crew member had emerged into a clear patch upon its three thick gliding appendage legs. It almost toppled but the longer, thinner tendrils with three digits stabilised its form by putting them into the shallow water to steady itself. The huge bulbous eyes were full of fear and the beak was open and panting for breath. Part of the partner's side was mashed and ripped open.

The creature hiding submerged in the lake could only watch the demise of the hunted fellow machine companion.

A biped might have thought the injured Martian looked like a huge, mutated tadpole's body with three tails being used as legs. Lots of little thin arms slithered like snakes, each with three slimy finger digits – a face like a raptor with beak, and huge bloated eyes the size of a biped's head.

Another shot rang out from within the mist and the Martian squealed and arched upon its three coiled legs. A biped's projectile had shot through the fog to hit the wretched companion. An explosion of bloody gore erupted from its front, the result of the speeding missile emerging from the flesh.

The fellow Martian companion fell against the trunk of the destroyed fighting machine – the false sanctuary it was pathetically trying to get back to, the debris of blood and gore slithering down the strange alloy into the murky lake water. The stricken companion never got the chance to slide along the messy armour and into the water.

The enraged bipeds emerged from the vapour in their strange face masks with large black lenses over their eyes and hanging ventilators, through which they seemed to breathe unhindered by the poison fog. They were adapting. Their projectile weapon sticks had long blades at the end. The vicious bipeds continued their charge and fell upon the wounded companion. All of the Earth creatures began to stab the near dead pilot with frenzied violence. There were no screams. The crew member was already spent of energy and lacked any will to fight back. It just glugged and choked as the stab wounds were inflicted upon its ample body mass. Resigned to this terrible stabbing, it quickly passed beyond its wretched life. Another biped came out of the black fog and called out in their strange noise. Immediately the bipeds stopped the assault. There were more noises and the watching Martian presumed these were more instructions. The bipeds then grabbed various areas of the dead companion's anatomy and dragged the corpse towards the smoke. Were the bipeds going to suck the remaining blood? The way Martians do? Perhaps the bipeds were not too dissimilar.

The one unarmed alien remained there, submerged and hidden by wisps of poison vapour, afraid it might be consumed by the bipeds. This was what the vile Earth things could do. Slowly the one surviving creature submerged itself and swam beneath the water, putting distance between itself and the carnage it had witnessed.

When the Martian finally surfaced to breathe, it was outside the area of the dark vapour. It could see and hear further shooting around another cluster of black fog. The other fighting machine had been felled and more bipeds were shooting inside that area of destruction. The bipeds had brought down two fighting machines. How could this be? There were more biped screams and shouts and the creature looked about for cover. It saw a small tower of red weed emerged from the water. There was a lone biped standing on a strange platform around it. The biped was alone and vulnerable, and it did not wear the second face. The artificial device thing hung loose upon the biped's chest. It had protruding lumps to the front and seemed slighter of build than the killer bipeds – it was the other type of gender common among all Earth species. This lone biped on the tower platform would be a target. Slowly the creature submerged and swam towards the strange stalk of red weed. It came up for breath and heard the shouts of other biped voices. The strange call meant nothing to the alien, but it sensed the noises were for the lone biped on the small red weed tower.

'We're coming back, Miss Clairmont. Please don't enter the water yet.'

CHAPTER 1

THE NEWSWORTHY EVENT

The steam train hissed to a halt at the pleasant rural railway station by Ring's End in the Fenlands of Cambridgeshire. The normally quiet farmland area was filled with people. Day trippers from March on one side, and Wisbech visitors on the other platform. All were milling around the surrounding fields, where an army of workmen were digging up one of the fields.

'I get the distinct impression that our precious snippet of news has gone on ahead of us, Mr Kenworthy,' said Rupert Percival as he climbed out of the train carriage onto the platform. He immediately put on his neat black bowler hat and heard a little boy call to his father.

'Dad, is that a grasshopper man?'

'No, don't be so loud, Freddie. It's rude to call out like that,' his father scolded, and they moved off along the platform.

Percival chuckled at the young lad's inquisitive nature and understood why the child thought him a grasshopper man.

'Should go for the old top hat out here, my good fellow,' said his companion, Humphrey Kenworthy. The man had stepped down to stand beside him and put on a top hat.

Percival smiled. 'Well, Mr Kenworthy. Perhaps I should have known better than to sport a bowler hat in the Fenlands where grasshopper men have mythical status, so I am told.'

Kenworthy looked about the train station and the viaduct rail bridge crossing the River Nene to Guyhirn village. 'There are more people here than I expected,' he said.

Percival looked along the platform and saw a ramp leading down to some level-crossing gates before the rails went onto the viaduct bridge, where the land dropped to a roadway. He pointed his walking stick. 'That way I believe, Mr Kenworthy.'

'Lead on, old chap. I'm right behind you.'

'The rail line goes across the Nene via the bridge to Guyhirn. Whereas the fields on this side is the place of all the commotion. Or at least, that is what I perceive it to be,' advised Percival.

'Well, you perceive away until your heart's content, old boy.' Kenworthy pressed his top hat down and followed. 'I hope we can find someone who can spread a little light on the matter before us. I'm sure there is a dashed good story here.'

'I must say, Mr Kenworthy, I do admire your optimism. I think this dashed War of the Worlds saga has flogged itself to death now. It's our employers that seem to be the ever-perusing gluttons for fresh information about the dreadful Martian invasion. It has been over for almost four years now and I still wonder when they will look for more diverse snippets of news.'

'By Jove our readers need it,' agreed Kenworthy. 'However, this one does seem to have revived that old stimulus. They seem to think there is such a fighting machine as the *Hereward* and they say the diggers are about to uncover the machine.'

Percival stopped in his stride and looked back. Kenworthy almost walked into him.

'What's wrong?' asked Kenworthy.

'You surely don't buy into that old Wake Men myth about the *Hereward*, do you?'

'Well of course I do,' replied Kenworthy. 'I have even received letters from the two station workers from this very station. They claim to have seen the very machine in action. In all its infamous glory, Mr Percival.'

'What two station workers?' asked Percival, looking put out that the information was only now being shared with him.

'Two rail workers from this very station were conscripted into the Wake Men Militia and were allowed into the piping system when the Martian advance swept over the Fenland. They were with a corporal and a private soldier. Men of the Cambridgeshire Yeomanry dispersed into the Wake Men Militia under the command of Colonel Henry Edward Blake – otherwise nicknamed Hereward Blake.'

'Blake of the Wake.' Percival laughed.

'No, Mr Percival, Hereward as in the Saxon outlaw who fought against the Norman conquerors – Hereward the Wake.'

'Yes, but his name is Blake and they call him Hereward Blake like Hereward of the Wake?' Percival raised an enquiring eyebrow.

'Trivialities, Mr Percival. Mere trivialities.' Kenworthy turned and resumed his walk.

'So where are these station worker chaps?' asked Percival, following Kenworthy. The man appeared to be armed with more information than he was letting on.

'Today they're off work and are waiting for me at the dig. I have my notebook, a beige top hat, a walking cane and the white carnation on my lapel.'

'I thought you were looking a tad spruced up, old boy. Why wait until now before letting me in on this?'

'Well, you are in on the whole matter, Mr Percival. I decided to wait until we got to the place first.'

'Oh well, I suppose I'd better let you in on my two exposés. Two soldiers of the Wake Men Militia are to meet me here. They haven't told me much. Never mentioned anything, except they were stationed at Observation Post Nine. Evidently, this position of the piping system saw a lot of action.'

'Well, my two railway workers were at Observation Post Nine. Perhaps they knew your Wake Men?' said Kenworthy, becoming more inquisitive.

The two men walked down the platform slope and turned to another drop road of gravel leading down to the lane, where a gate opened out onto a muddy water-drenched field.

'I say, our shoes are going to get awful messy, old boy.' Percival looked to a man sitting at a horse and cart. 'How much to take us out to the dig, my good man?'

'A shilling,' replied the man with several people already sitting on board. Then he added, 'A shilling, each.'

Percival was about to remonstrate. He felt sure the ordinary folk of the Fens who were sitting on the cart had not been ripped off for a shilling and was about to say so. However, Kenworthy's restraining hand gripped his elbow.

'Not now, Mr Percival,' said Kenworthy with a smile. He put his hand in his pocket and produced two one-shilling pieces, which he promptly dropped into the cartman's hand. He turned to Percival and smiled. 'Let's not stand on ceremony, my dear Mr Percival.'

Both men climbed onto the cart and sat among the local fenland people as the horse and cart moved forward into the field. All around were groups of people traipsing over the muddy field towards the dig, where hordes of workmen and soldiers were uncovering a site of former battle.

Kenworthy was now the reporter bristling with confidence and leading the way. Percival felt as though he had taken a drop of importance since leaving the train full of enthusiasm and a sense of self-importance. It was the fact that Kenworthy had kept his source secret and was unperturbed by Percival's secret source. Almost as though he knew about his two soldiers before being supposedly enlightened. Kenworthy was a reporter one step in front of him and Percival had only just discovered it.

'I say, Kenworthy. You didn't seem surprised by my two soldier contacts,' he asked sullenly.

'Well, Mike Green and Bill Ackerman told me of the former Corporal Wickham and Private Parker who were meeting with their own reporter chap from the *Express*. I naturally assumed it to be you. My chaps and yours were over the moon that they would get to meet back here. It's like a grand day out for them. A trip down memory lane, so to speak.'

'Oh,' replied Percival.

'Don't let it take the wind out of your sails, old boy. Our sources have played us off together, you know. They want a good pub lunch and a few pints to boot out of all this. They're going to give us an up-front story of the Wake Men and the *Hereward*, you know.'

Percival sighed. 'Well, since you put it like that, then a little sumptuous repast is not too much to ask on their part.'

'Cheap at half the price,' agreed Kenworthy.

The cart jostled over the wet lumpy turf as Kenworthy pointed his cane out in the direction of the raised embankment, where distant Dutch engineers were working about. 'Much of this area is reclaimed land. The Dutch built the dike systems some centuries back, I'm led to believe. The flood ditches in these surrounding fields fill up with water first if the river breaches the raised banks and floods into the fields. I think it was begun in Henry the Eighth's time. Don't quote me on that, it's just hearsay. But now the Dutch are back repairing the breach made by Colonel Blake, just prior to the Martian fighting machines coming here. The Wake

Men had laid a piping system along and within the flood ditches. Big pipes snuggly fitting in the drops that were big enough for people to traverse.'

'Yes, I've been told this too. A rather ingenious plan, by all accounts,' Percival acknowledged.

Kenworthy chuckled. 'Fenland people like to brag that they brought down more fighting machines than any other part of the country. Observation Post Nine, the place this old cart is pulling us to, accounts for most of that. All due to an underwater piping network.'

At the dig area, there were people milling about all around the barriers. A few policemen had put up a tape barrier that was successfully keeping the crowd from becoming too intrusive and hampering the excavation site.

The horse and cart came to a stop as the passengers aboard started to climb down via a wooden step to the rear. They sauntered off into the melee of onlookers. There were a few overweight older ladies that needed considerable assistance getting off the cart. Kenworthy and Percival waited patiently until all were off-loaded. Once this was done, Kenworthy and Percival climbed down to see two men standing with two soldiers in khaki beige uniform and pith helmets.

'Ah!' Kenworthy held out his hand to the two men dressed in civilian clothes and let them have one of his big beaming smiles. 'Mr Michael Green and Mr William Ackerman, I presume.'

Percival moved forward to his two soldiers. 'Sergeant Wickham and Corporal Parker, I would presume.' He also smiled and shook each soldier's hand very warmly.

'I'm Mike Green,' one of the men said, smiling back, and shook Kenworthy's hand. 'Very pleased to meet you.'

'And I'm Bill Ackerman,' the other corrected politely and clasped Kenworthy's hand once he had finished with Mike. 'We're out of railway uniform on account of being allowed a day off to meet you, the newspaper man.'

'Oh, yes,' agreed Mike. 'Our employers are thrilled that our little train station at Ring's End will be in the national newspaper. You will mention the station won't you, Mr Kenworthy.'

'Indeed, I will, kind Sirs. It should be my privilege to do so.' Again, Kenworthy gave his two information sources his best gratifying smile.

Sergeant Wickham spoke next: 'I think you two newspaper chaps have arrived just in time. The workmen have erected another two scaffold towers either side of the *Hereward*. She's been buried under mud and water for some time now, but the diggers have cleared enough mud and silt for us to hoist up the burnt-out hull of the fighting machine.'

9

'By Jove, that sounds splendid,' replied Percival. 'Let's see if we can work our way to the front.'

'I think we might be able to do a little better than that, Sir. My captain has given me leave to allow Mike, Bill, Mr Kenworthy and your good self to come with Corporal Parker and I beyond the barrier markings and into the actual dig. The hoists are all in place and the raise will commence at any moment now.'

'Oh splendid,' replied Kenworthy.

Corporal Parker spoke next: 'I would ask you gentlemen to try and walk on the crude palisade path we have laid. It will stop you getting your shoes all muddy.'

'Sound advice,' replied Percival. 'Thank you, Corporal Parker.'

With no further idle talk, the two reporters followed the soldiers and the off-duty rail workers. A policeman lifted the barrier tape and allowed all six individuals through. They gingerly walked along the wooden palisade towards the workmen. All about were the derelict hulks of Martian fighting machines. It was an eerie sensation but also gratifying to see the vile mechanical contrivances as broken relics, useless battered alien alloy rusting away in the mud.

'Good Lord! There are a fair few of the blighters lying scattered about,' Kenworthy muttered in genuine surprise.

'There certainly are,' Percival replied. He looked back to Mike and Bill, the station workers. 'Did you chaps witness any of this?'

'We did, Mr Percival,' Bill answered.

'What ones did you see destroyed?' added Kenworthy.

'All of them.' Mike was very matter of fact.

Sergeant Wickham stopped and held out a hand to the reporters who went to stand among local dignitaries, all of whom had secured special vantage points for themselves. The raising of the *Hereward* would become a special feature in local folklore. A little alcove in history and a major event in the quiet Fenlands.

As Kenworthy and Percival stood beside a local councillor, they watched the sergeant wave at an officer who was standing on a mound with a few ground workers. The smartly dressed captain called down to someone obscured by the mud mound.

'Do you know, Mr Kenworthy,' whispered Percival, 'I think they were waiting for us especially.'

'I think you are correct, Mr Percival. Look, there are a few cameramen with tripods over there.'

'Tripods that hold cameras.' Percival chuckled. 'Not Martians. Don't say that too loudly, old chap. Likely to frighten and upset the local Fenlanders.'

A few commands were issued and the stress ropes attached to the scaffold towers began to go taut. The many pulley systems under stress began to squeak, the disturbed sludge, hidden behind the mound, began to make all manner of squelching noises in protest. Further back, beyond the police barrier, the crowded audience murmured in collective awe. The muddied capsule was gradually being prised free of the restraining muck.

The humming crowd's amazement grew with intensity, their excited chatter informing the closer dignitaries, obscured from the immediate event, of the compelling sight unfolding before them.

'You know, Mr Kenworthy, I think the people beyond the barrier in their cheap seats have a better vantage point. That mound is in our way...' Percival stopped his chatter as the giant Martian container began to rise above the bank and into clear view. Wet mud cascaded down the curved hull, the thick clumps falling back to the earth.

'Good Lord,' muttered Kenworthy.

A fireman began to spray the elevated case with a fire hose. Behind the man, other volunteers were working the fire engine cart by hand – four men vigorously pumping their bar handles up and down to get a hearty water pressure.

The concentrated spray whooshed out of the nozzle and was immediately aimed at the top of the alien alloy. The water cascading down gradually caused the thick grime to wash away and fall with the new and more intense downpour.

Now the dignitaries could see the entire event held up before them. The crowd were like spectators at an elaborate circus event. A Martian machine of difference. There were derelict Martian titans rotting the length and breadth of the country, but this one was different. This was the legendary *Hereward*. It was special. Very special.

'Do you think they'll have this one in a museum?' asked Kenworthy.

Suddenly the crowd, beyond the barrier, roared in a gathering of awed delight. Slowly, the *Hereward* began to turn. As the giant capsule rotated, its blind side came around into the view of the dignitaries. They saw the faded and dirty drenched flag of the Union Jack, plastered against the hull. The two top corners of the flag were fixed to the casing as was one of the bottom corners. The lower left fluttered freely in the breeze. The black painted words 'Hereward' could be seen beneath the flag.

Percival looked to Sergeant Wickham. 'Does that bring back memories?'

The sergeant looked directly at the reporter and replied, 'Yes, Mr Percival. I'm afraid it does. Very sad ones and rather precious recollections too.'

'I say, I'm dashed sorry, Sergeant Wickham. Never meant to open old wounds and all…'

'That's fine, Mr Percival.' Wickham smiled reassuringly back.

As Percival looked about, he realised that Corporal Parker, Mike Green and Bill Ackerman were all looking equally as sad. There were strange and perhaps diabolical memories swirling in each man's head. He then looked to Kenworthy who was staring straight back at him. The reporters knew there was a story to be told here and they were standing with four witnesses to the events that happened during the War of the Worlds.

'May we know more of your stories?' asked Kenworthy sincerely. 'We should like to put them in our newspapers.'

'Historical events such as this must be told,' said Percival in support.

'Where would we begin?' Mike was looking at Sergeant Wickham.

'I suppose the train station on that final day, just before the last train and the arrival of the Martians,' began Sergeant Wickham.

'Yes,' said Parker. 'I was the rank of private and you the corporal.'

'That's right.' Bill smiled.

'Events moved at a very quick pace from that afternoon,' said Mike. 'Never known things to change so fast as on that very day when we were standing back over there on that train platform.'

CHAPTER 2

THE FORCED CONSCRIPTION OF POTENTIAL MEDICAL STAFF (JULY 1898)

Two soldiers of the Cambridgeshire Yeomanry stood upon the train platform with two railway station staff. All four concerned men looked south west to the glowing red hue of the horizon. The wicked radiance stretched for miles across the flat, reddened Fens of Cambridgeshire – the red glow of the Martian vegetation that spread quicker than the Martians could advance, leaving the air with a sweet tang of a disturbing alien aroma.

Further off, beyond the wicked vista, came the bellow of artillery. The doubtful *boom, boom* of desperate and failing human resistance, unseen men trying to stop the strange Martians concealed in their tripod machines. From the rumours the four men had heard, the aliens were repulsive. Vile extra-terrestrials in giant stalking mechanisms.

Between the shots of cannon fire came an evil and more diabolical sound – the nerve-raking far-off screech of strange and deadly heat ray. The shocking response to desperate and pathetic human resistance. Here and there came terrifying Martian war cries, fanning out over the Fens.

'They're still far off,' muttered the young station hand nervously. The soldiers had come to know the young man as Bill.

'Yet getting louder, mile by mile,' replied Private Parker of the Cambridgeshire Yeomanry. He was around the same age as Bill. The lads had developed a rapport and friendship.

Mike, the older station worker spoke next: 'Formations of giant Martian machine monsters from out of space stalking across the land, moving ever closer to our little rail station.'

'Who would believe such a thing,' replied Parker.

'Aye, and at Ring's End, so close to home,' added Bill. 'It's hard to believe.'

'A most worrying situation indeed,' said Mike. The man was almost trembling with fear and his bulbous nose twitched above his bushy moustache. He looked down at the freight order sheet he was holding. 'The last scheduled delivery of pipes is coming in. We'll be signing off today at 13.15. By tomorrow this place will be deserted. It could be overrun by these Martian machine creatures. I wonder if this schedule sheet should be put in a place of prominence. Maybe one day men will return and it'll be a thing of interest to historical sorts.'

'I think that is the least of our concerns. Calling it "a worrying situation" is putting it mildly, Mike,' replied Bill, equally as anxious. 'Very mildly, to be honest. As for machine creatures, I think the monsters are inside the machines.'

'They are, indeed? I wish we could own such machines,' Mike responded as he put his pipe to his mouth. His hands were shaking as he tried to light the packed tobacco.

'Aye,' replied Bill. 'Give the Martian things something to think about, that would.'

'Would even out the odds good and proper.' Mike looked towards the glow on the horizon and squeezed a droplet of joy from his little fantasy.

'It's those sounds of heat rays,' added Private Parker. He looked to Corporal Wickham and continued, 'That hideous screeching goes right through a bloke. I wish I knew why we're still here. We've been living in that station hut for almost two weeks now. Just watching blooming passenger trains full of people, plus freight trains for those blooming cattle carts that take that giant piping out across the blooming Fens. Our once green Fens that we've watched turn red. I wish our great leaders would let us know what they're doing with all those sections of giant pipes. I bet the red weed is growing around those pipes they're laying, it's smothering everything. The carts just keep pulling those blooming pipes out into the red fields. I can hear all the banging and shouting, but I can't tell what our lads are doing. Why are we still here? Why is no one telling us what's going on?'

Mike ignored Parker's moaning about the pipe sections. Parker was always going on about it. The primary concern was the approaching Martians. He cursed: 'Heat rays is a sound that'll be getting louder as this Martian fighting machine army continues. Who would imagine folk like us ever having such a mad conversation? Invading Martians from out of space. A War of the Worlds! Our world and theirs.' He looked at the outbuildings on the station platform and noted the spread of red weed over the brickwork. 'Bloody red weed is getting everywhere. But it's the least of our worries.'

Corporal Wickham had been silent, but now decided to add his opinion. 'It'll not be long now.' He clutched his rifle barrel with the stock resting on the platform against his foot. His free hand caressed his gas mask. Soon they might need to put them on. 'We'll not be going anywhere, Parker. Soldiers coming here to board the last train? It's a dream, mate. It's not going to happen. Besides, any passenger train will be packed out with civilians. They'll be no room for us. Use your blooming common sense, lad. We're going nowhere near the coast.'

Private Parker sighed nervously. 'I can't understand why they won't let us board that last passenger train to Spalding when it gets here. There's nothing more the four of us can do. I was hoping our great guard stint would end today with that last passenger train. But the troops are still out there somewhere. They should be getting ready to board the last train here, too. One especially for us. Our Yeomanry should be here now, ready to leave.'

'Will you get the picture, Parker? Our lads are not coming to board any train. And our toil and woe has not begun yet. I think we're getting ready to make a stand here.'

'I know.' Parker sighed, clutching the loose gas mask hanging around his neck. 'And I suppose we'll be wearing these things.' He looked at the two station workers with their gas masks hanging loose. He noted their dishevelled rail uniforms too. Mike and Bill were on permanent duty with them. Just observers that were not allowed to leave the small rail station. 'I had been hoping we could get on the last train.'

'We have noticed,' replied Corporal Wickham sarcastically.

'Well, it won't be this train coming along, lad,' said Bill, looking at an approaching steam engine in the distance, coming along the line towards them from the direction of March town and away from the panoramic violent red glow of the horizon.

'It's another freight with more piping,' added Mike. 'More carriages from March yard. There are loads of these pipeline segments stored there. I think they're storing them in other places too. Scattered storage, I think, all around the Fens.'

'There are also more cattle wagons coming to off-load and take the pipes out into the fields.' Bill pointed at a convoy of cattle-drawn carts being led across the fields towards the station by engineers of the Cambridgeshire Yeomanry.

More military engineers suddenly appeared from the train station's building, on the opposite platform. Engineers and soldiers to man the huge pulley systems where the freight train would halt.

'More of those huge pipes to load onto the cattle carts. Why do they keep taking the pipes out into the Fens?' asked Mike.

'Yes,' said Parker. 'Why do we need more of those huge pipe parts? There must be loads of them now. What has our Colonel Hereward Blake got into his head about the mad pipelines he keeps laying in the flood ditches?'

Corporal Wickham answered, 'They're laying them and bolting them together, then using some sort of tar to seal them – every pipe all along the flood trenches of the fields. This piping is big enough for people to scurry along out of sight. Out of sight of the Martians.' He looked at Parker and raised an eyebrow. 'I know the colonel has the nickname of Hereward Blake, but it's Colonel Henry Edward Blake for real. The "Hereward" part is because of Hereward the Wake who found refuge here back in the days of William the Conqueror.'

'And now the Cambridgeshire Yeomanry is being called Wake Men,' added Parker. He nodded at Mike and Bill. 'Ask the rail staff.'

Corporal Wickham smiled at the sheepish station workers. 'Wake Men, aye? I like the sound of that. So, we are Colonel Hereward Blake's Wake Men, are we? Let's hope we can be as good as old Hereward the Wake then, shall we? Perhaps cause problems for the Martians the way Hereward did the Normans.'

Parker looked dismayed. 'I don't like the sound of that, Corp. That's why I was hoping we'd be going with the last passenger train to Spalding. Don't forget, Hereward the Wake lost. The blooming Normans won, in the end. Our Colonel Hereward Blake is probably one of King William's offspring.'

Wickham raised an eyebrow in amusement. 'Well, perhaps our Colonel Hereward will win, and we can still be good Wake Men for him. And I wish to repeat! No, lad! For the final time, we are not getting on the last train. So, please stop going on about it and give us all a rest on the matter. I think we're going to be living under the water inside those blooming pipes. Why do you think all those mining air-circulation contraptions have come into the station a few days back? What do you think the scattered conning towers are for? They're for observers watching out for Martian fighting machines. Why do you suppose all that telephone cable has come from that strange Swedish communication company? That's telephone wire to speak through. All these pipes in the flood ditches are forming a vast, gigantic spoked wheel. Imagine this spoked wheel of pipes is a big spiderweb of tunnels for us to move through. The big square water tanks and conning towers are observation posts, and with telephones and telegram wires we can keep all of our, er...' He smiled at the station workers and continued, 'Our Wake Men fully up to date with Martian movement. Where and when. Up to the moment.'

'What!' exclaimed Parker. The young soldier was flabbergasted. 'Do you mean to say we are not leaving in any way whatsoever? Not even marching somewhere. How long as this been planned out?'

'Almost as long as the government began to realise the Martians were going to attack across the land, I would imagine. That was almost straight away. Colonel Blake could commandeer a great many things and chose the Fenlands as a base where we might be able to fight the Martians in a more cunning manner. In this area, the government gave our colonel the reins, so to speak.'

'Yes, while the government packed up and buggered off to Edinburgh,' hissed Parker.

'How long have you known about this tunnel business?' asked Mike.

'Well, I haven't been told. I'm just a corporal. High-ranking officers do not disclose such information to me, but I have noticed the way the piping system has been laid out over the weeks. Surely you chaps have too?'

'I did wonder,' replied Bill.

They barely noticed the steam engine screech to a halt as it rumbled in and stopped at Ring's End station on the opposite platform. There was nothing unusual with the freight train, except it would be the last. More piping was stacked on the freight carriages.

The pulley systems on the opposite platform went into immediate action while the cattle wagons were brought up onto the raised stand via the level crossing. Military workers suddenly appeared from buildings and around the cattle wagons. They called out instructions to one another as the huge piping was hoisted from the rail carriages by the wooden pulley systems.

Parker was staring at the familiar sight with new open-mouthed shock. 'I never realised they were doing things like that. Building tunnels! Even though I've been watching this for two weeks now, I never questioned why. I was concentrating too much on the hope of us getting to King's Lynn or Spalding.'

'Well, I'm going to have to repeat myself. I'm sorry to disappoint you, Parker, but you are a Wake Man now. Our Cambridgeshire Yeomanry with all the other added groups are a new fenland militia. A little army that's going to take on the Martian fighting machines, lad.' Wickham smiled, winked, and then added, 'You might as well get used to it.'

'What is that for?' asked Parker, pointing at a huge rectangular water tank. It was steadfastly fastened to one of the rail carriages and soldiers were climbing over it. They were unfastening various tethers.

Wickham snorted and answered, 'The pipes that run along the flood ditches go into the sides of tanks, such as this one – underground corridors going into rooms, so to speak. There have been a number of them brought in over the past few days. They make for small office rooms below the ground. The flood ditches have been widened in these areas to accommodate the mass of these water tanks. They're known as observation posts. I'm told there are at least twenty-six observation posts scattered about the network of piping so far. Maybe this water tank will get to be Observation Post Twenty-seven, though I can't see how they can get that one in place before the dike embankment is blown.'

Parker looked shocked. 'That water tank is huge. It's meant to keep water in, not out.'

Mike commented, 'Well, many things are adapted for different uses. If the tank can keep water in, a hollow one may keep water out.'

'This is so,' agreed Wickham as he pointed to the huge water container. 'And above the tank you'll notice the circular conning tower. That will always be above the water while the observation area remains below, once the fen is flooded. You'll notice the lookout slits?' He pointed to the top of the cone tower on the water tank.

'Wide at the bottom and narrower at the top,' added Parker, scrutinising the upper lookout tower. 'Like a witch's hat.'

'The square cistern area is big enough,' gasped Bill. 'It must be eight feet high, maybe nine feet.'

Wickham smiled and added, 'Ten feet square – length and width. A height of nine feet plus a small gantry platform at the bottom of the coned tower – where the wider upper part is. Allows observation men to stand comfortably above the tank's floor area. Has a ladder down to the office area.'

'How are we going to fight Martians inside these pipes that are buried in flood trenches?' asked Parker, looking rather concerned. Another distant Martian war cry sounded off towards the south west. 'Blimey, they're getting closer.'

'I noticed explosive engineers working along the embankment of the River Nene as it goes to Wisbech,' said Mike. 'They're going to blow the dike's embankment holding the River Nene, aren't they?' He looked out over the fen. 'That will definitely flood the place.'

Wickham nodded in agreement. 'Yes, I think so.'

'That will do the job. All of the fields will be underwater,' replied Bill. 'Only the conning towers will be above and everyone else will be under the flooded Fens in the pipe system. I see what the colonel is trying to do now.'

'That is rather clever,' admitted Mike.

Again, Wickham smiled. 'Some of the engineers have been laying mines and lassoing trip ropes in the fields. They have sliding rule systems to tighten and relay at will. If you all think carefully, it starts to form a picture in the mind's eye. It certainly did for me, some time back. I could only get the odd snippet of information from the engineers, but I think they know what's going on. Considerably more than they let on. Why do you think we're all issued with these good-quality gas masks? Every soldier and rail worker has them.'

Parker remained spellbound with astonishment. 'We're going to try and trap Martians in the flooded Fens?' He watched the engineers unloading the piping via the pulley systems. Everything was being done at speed and precision. As soon as a cart was loaded the cattle moved off with their loads – back down the train platform slope to cross the line in front of the steam engine, through the level crossing's raised gates and out into the lane, then through a farm gate and across the pasture, out into the Fens.

'It's been going on right under our blooming noses and I never noticed,' said the enlightened Bill.

Parker was now visibly disappointed. 'I knew something was going to go wrong with my notion of leaving this place. Are we going to be luring these blooming great fighting machines into the flooded fen? It will be like a little puddle to giant contraptions like Martian tripods.'

'Hold up there, lads,' said Wickham. 'We have a lieutenant and two grasshopper men coming this way.'

'Well, it was becoming a nasty conversation anyway,' replied Parker, sulking at his new-found knowledge.

'What are grasshopper men?' asked Bill.

'Grasshopper men from the universities in Cambridge,' answered Parker.

Wickham added, 'The blokes in the bowler hats and gas masks are nicknamed "grasshopper men". They started putting their gas masks on as soon as they left the Cambridge University colleges. That with their bowler hats. All university admin men are obliged to wear bowler hats on duty at the colleges when the students are about the grounds. They kept that tradition when on duty here with the new Wake Men Militia. Plus, they've added to it with the obliged wearing of gas masks too. It gives them a creepy anonymity.'

'What's anonymity?' asked Parker.

'It means you don't know who the bugger is,' added Mike.

'You'll know they are grasshopper men,' replied Wickham. 'That should do nicely.'

'So, all bowler hats and gasmasked men are the university admin staff from Cambridge?' replied Mike. 'They all look strange in their chest waders, ties, gas masks and bowler hats. I don't know who are scarier. The Martians or the grasshopper men?'

Corporal Wickham and Private Parker shouldered their arms, stood to attention, and saluted as the young lieutenant stopped before them.

'As you were, men,' said the officer. 'I'm sorry this is all very rushed indeed. I need a little backup and require you two chaps to board the last passenger train to Spalding with me.' The officer noticed a look of excited hope on Private Parker's face and then added, 'We will not be going with it to Spalding. We just need to bring two passengers off the train. I must bring you two chaps back with me upon the forced conscription of two train passengers. Sorry, this is all rather rushed but we are on a very tight schedule. You are to be part of my observation unit back in the pipe system. I've been told to requisition the two soldiers at the station, meaning you two chaps, and to apprehend two passengers on the next and last train coming along the lines.'

'Yes, Sir,' replied Wickham, standing back at ease.

'Right then, Corporal. I have two university admin chaps with me because they know the particular doctor we are to apprehend. He works at Jesus College where these two university admins worked.'

'I see, Sir.' Wickham wanted to ask why the person was to be apprehended, but thought it overreaching his authority with an officer.

As though sensing the awkward dilemma, the young officer smiled. 'I'm Lieutenant Paige and I'm here to conscript a certain Dr Cheema into our new Wake Men Militia. He and his lab assistant Miss Clairmont are needed for their medical knowledge. A couple of dissecting types that cut up dead things and find out what killed them. All that sort of rot, if you get my drift.'

'Oh, I see, Sir. I understand. Are we going to conscript a lady too, Sir?'

'Indeed we are, Corporal…'

'I do beg your pardon, Sir. I'm Corporal Wickham.'

Lieutenant Paige's neat, thin moustache rose into a polite smile. 'Yes, we need Miss Clairmont too, Corporal Wickham. She's a lab assistant of good quality and has assisted Dr Cheema in his teaching duties at Jesus College for some time, so I'm told. They each have family waiting to board one of the many small vessels at Wisbech, a small craft to go up the Nene and out into the Wash. Dr Cheema's wife and two daughters are waiting in the small customs hut as we speak. They have been temporarily apprehended but spaces aboard a vessel are reserved for them upon Dr Cheema's compliance. Also, for his assistant. We have Miss Clairmont's mother in the same customs hut under the same condition – a reserved place upon a vessel upon Miss Clairmont's compliance.'

'I see, Sir,' replied Wickham. 'How can we communicate with the customs men at Wisbech?'

'Oh, we have lots of telephone cable. Colonel Blake saw to that. The first observation post of our tunnel network has a telephone. It's just across the field, over there. All observation posts are now equipped with telephones and telegrams. There is a link exchange to contact the quayside in Wisbech. The doctor and Miss Clairmont will have the gratification of being able to speak with their relatives.' Lieutenant Paige looked about the station platform. 'Would have been worthwhile running wire out to this station too. Might have made it easier to persuade the two people we must apprehend and conscript into the Wake Men Militia service.'

'The passenger train's coming along the line, Sir,' said Mike, the older station worker.

A whistle blew on the opposite platform where the unloading of piping was complete. The pulley systems were wheeled away from the stationary freight train. The last cattle cart carrying the large piping sections rumbled away, past the level crossing. Then the gates were closed. Slowly the steam engine pulled the empty carriages away and moved off towards the next station, leaving room for the incoming passenger train.

'Right then, men,' said Lieutenant Paige to the two soldiers. 'Follow me and the university admin men. Dr Cheema will be rather easy to recognise. He's a very tall Sikh man of around six foot four. He's also in turban headwear.'

'I see, Sir,' replied Wickham as they left the two station workers, Mike and Bill, and followed the lieutenant over the level crossing planks to the opposite platform and the incoming passenger train.

CHAPTER 3

DR CHEEMA AND HIS ASSISTANT LAB WORKER

Miss Clairmont and Dr Cheema had no idea what was about to become of them when they were standing in the packed carriage as it rumbled along the tracks towards Guyhirn. All around them were people from all walks of life – rich people, poor people. No more was first class or second class very noticeable. Gone were the social protocols of polite British society. People just sat and stood wherever they could board the train. The Indian doctor towered above everyone, with his tall frame complemented by a huge green turban. He certainly stood out in the packed carriage.

'Not far now, Miss Clairmont,' Dr Cheema leaned down and whispered politely. 'I think we're away from the recruiting militia. I was a little worried back in Cambridge. I thought we were to be forcefully conscripted. They might have wanted us to work in the field for them.'

Dr Cheema stood upright when he had finished murmuring his minor conclusion. He looked over the heads of the many people, desperate individuals who were looking a little less frightened. Perhaps a slight air of gratification was settling over the fleeing people. The doctor supposed it was natural. At one point, when the train pulled out of Cambridge and into the surrounding countryside, they had witnessed a giant Martian tripod in the distance. The dreadful fighting machine was striding over the meadows. Thankfully, it seemed uninterested in the train. To every passenger's relief, the rail line veered away and continued into an area not yet overrun by the Martian advance.

Twenty-six-year-old Miss Clairmont looked about her. Her raven hair was in an updo and some of the strands hung down the side of her face. The raven hair stood out against her soft, pale porcelain skin and striking blue eyes. She looked up to nervously whisper back. This time, Dr Cheema leaned down to listen.

'I think we were able to board the train because the Martian machines had reached the outskirts of Cambridge,' she began. 'The authorities at the station were leaving because they had to face the

Martian attack. I don't know what they could possibly have done, God bless them. Perhaps they bought this train some time to escape.'

'Very noble men indeed, Miss Clairmont,' Dr Cheema agreed.

'I wonder if any of them have survived?'

'I was a little surprised we were not apprehended, Miss Clairmont. Because of our occupations, I thought the army may have conscripted us into one of their medical units. After all, our professions would be of use in some field hospitals,' said Dr Cheema quietly. 'I've heard of other medical teachers and students being recruited.'

'I can't imagine of what importance we could be to the armed forces of today, Dr Cheema,' replied Miss Clairmont. 'Your doctorate is in infectious pathogens – mainly via autopsy. And although I'm your lab assistant, my original field of study is more towards veterinary pathology. I don't think there's much use for cavalry in this war of the worlds conflict. Martians are not intimidated by our cavalry. Our limited knowledge on human biology would probably be of minor use. If the military forces were desperate, but I doubt there's much time to think of such things under the more anxious circumstances we find ourselves in. Not now, at least. We'll soon be at Wisbech and your wife and daughters will be there to greet you.'

Dr Cheema smiled. 'And your mother's waiting for you, Miss Clairmont. I'm sure we will all feel most gratified when that precious moment comes.'

'That last station we passed through was March. We are well and truly in the Fenlands now, but the red weed is even out this far. Look at the fields.'

Dr Cheema agreed. 'The pastures are just as red out here. I just want to be as far away from this place as possible.'

'Wisbech is not far. I think the train then moves on to Spalding.' Miss Clairmont was still nervous as she continued to look out onto the unnatural red Fens, but she felt the worst was behind them. For the time being.

'Well, not long now, Miss Clairmont, I'm sure.' Dr Cheema smiled reassuringly.

The train began to slow down as they approached another station. Someone muttered that it was Ring's End station for Guyhirn.

'There seems to be a lot of activity in the fields. Lots of soldiers moving about in scattered groups,' said Dr Cheema, peering over heads and out of the carriage window.

'Perhaps new army defence positions?' replied Miss Clairmont. She was ignorant of army things but felt a guess might be in order. The small talk helped settle the nerves of the trauma they had recently been through.

'I can't understand why,' replied Dr Cheema in a low voice. 'This is Fenland. Very flat and very difficult to hold against giant fighting machines. Nowhere to hide or take cover.'

The train halted at the platform and there were murmurings of concern among the many passengers. They heard an old woman ask questions of others.

'Why are those strange men wearing big chest waders with gas masks and bowler hats?'

Instantly Miss Clairmont looked up at Dr Cheema. 'Bowler hats?' she said. 'Why are soldiers in bowler hats? Perhaps she means pith helmets.'

Dr Cheema looked confused and a little nervous. 'Some of the college admin staff went with the army. They could be from the university colleges. Many came out this way with the Cambridgeshire Yeomanry.'

Everyone looked to the end of the train carriage as three soldiers wearing sand-coloured pith helmets stepped up into the carriage. One officer, a corporal and a private soldier. The two soldiers had their rifles shouldered and didn't seem threatening in any way. The officer's pistol was holstered, and he showed no sign of threat either. However, it was the two men who followed with faces hidden beneath gas masks with dark lenses. They looked like people with grasshopper heads wearing bowler hats.

One cocky man said as much: 'Who are the grasshopper men?'

There followed an eerie silence. Every person on the train went mute. The soldiers they could understand, but the strange men in gas masks with dark eye shields looked like mysterious humanoid abominations. Their hissing breath through the gas masks added to the eerie revelation of diabolical authority. All the passengers watched as one of the grasshopper men slowly pointed a finger at Dr Cheema.

The university admin man turned back to Lieutenant Paige and looking at him through the dark lenses of his gas mask, nodded compliantly while still pointing towards the tall Sikh man at the end of the train carriage.

'Dr Cheema and Miss Clairmont, I presume,' said the young officer with a polite smile. 'I'm Lieutenant Paige. There is no cause for concern. We need you to disembark this train. Your wife, daughters, and Miss Clairmont's mother are waiting to talk with you. Please come with us. You'll be speaking with them in moments.'

Immediately, Dr Cheema and Miss Clairmont pushed through the throng of people to open the carriage door and stepped down onto the platform. Each wore a look of concern and both were very confused. The sickly-sweet smell of red weed seemed more intense in the open. The out-house buildings had creeping red weed clinging to the bottom of the brickwork and the alien parasitical weed was gradually spreading upwards like a strange wild red ivy.

'What on Earth is going on?' muttered Miss Clairmont. Her voice was nervous, and she wanted some form of consolation.

'I'm not sure, Miss Clairmont, but these soldiers know who we are and of our relatives. They must have information for us,' assured Dr Cheema.

The three soldiers and the two grasshopper men got off the train carriage too. The officer turned to the front of the train and raised his arm for the train driver to proceed. The train kicked back into life and slowly pulled away from the station.

'Wait!' said Dr Cheema. 'Why is the train leaving?'

'What's going on?' exclaimed Miss Clairmont in panic. The concern on her face obscured the sweat and discomfort she obtained on the packed train.

She noticed Corporal Wickham looking at her with a touch of concern. It made her feel worse and more frightened. 'Please tell us where our relatives are. You said they were here?'

'You are being taken to talk with them, Miss Clairmont,' added Lieutenant Paige. 'Please follow me and I can promise that you will be speaking with them very soon. Please, follow me.'

Lieutenant Paige abruptly turned and began to walk along the platform. The train was moving off to the east over the bizarre red Fenland.

'Why does he keep saying "speaking", as opposed to "seeing"?' asked Miss Clairmont, following the officer.

'There is something strange about his wording,' agreed Dr Cheema in hushed tones as he walked beside her. 'Something is insincere, and when soldiers say there is no cause for concern, it usually means the opposite. I knew we might be required for something. They need our specialities. I just knew it.'

'What use can we be to them with our knowledge of animal autopsy and pathogens?' Miss Clairmont frowned.

'Perhaps we are their best bet if they have a Martian corpse?' suggested Dr Cheema.

'Do you really think so?' replied Miss Clairmont nervously.

'It's the only explanation I can think of. Unless they think we do people.' Dr Cheema sighed resignedly.

'They seem in an awful hurry, and I don't think they know we just do experimental classroom autopsies,' agreed Miss Clairmont.

'I'm sure they may do, Miss Clairmont. That may be why they want us,' he added.

'Do you really think they want us to dissect a Martian?' asked Miss Clairmont.

Private Parker overheard some of the chatter and fell back with Corporal Wickham. 'I think the doctor and his assistant have smelt a rat,' he said.

'Of course, the doctor has smelt a big rodent. It comes with the territory when voices of authority start practising their fine art of understatement,' whispered Wickham. 'And our doctor and assistant can tell when a bit of John Bull is in the wind.'

'That's a nice polite way of putting it, Corporal. I hope it muffles the smell of this blooming red weed,' added Parker sarcastically.

'Careful there, Parker.' Wickham raised an eyebrow mockingly with a slight hint of humour. Humour that should not be pushed too far.

Another barrage of distant guns boomed, and all stopped momentarily and looked back at the red sky to the south. More screeches of the heat ray and the further distant bellow of the horned Martian battle cry. It fanned out over the red Fens.

'Dr Cheema, Miss Clairmont, please speed up. The engineers are about to blow the dike walls of the River Nene soon. This whole area will be flooded. They're just waiting for the train to reach Wisbech and move on, then the explosives will be detonated. This whole area will soon be below the waterline.'

The two station workers, Mike and Bill, came out from one of the buildings. Mike called out, 'There are no more trains now, Sir. That was the last one.'

'Yes, you chaps will need to come with us too. Soon this area will be flooded,' called Lieutenant Paige. The officer had forgotten about the rail staff and now he was making it up as he went along.

'Can't we go home?' asked Bill.

'It would be unadvisable. Your families have left on boats some days ago, I believe.' Lieutenant Paige was frowning at the station hands.

'Well yes, Sir. The Wake Men allowed it. On condition we stayed here to work the trains coming and going,' replied Mike.

'That's right.' Lieutenant Paige smiled. 'Now you can come into the piping or take your chances over land. I would strongly advise you to join us.'

The two station hands looked at one another and then quickly decided to comply and follow the group. Each man was resigned to the uncanny situation. They fell in next to Corporal Wickham and Private Parker.

'I had a funny feeling something like this was going to happen,' said Bill. 'At least my wife and kids got away on the boat.'

Miss Clairmont fell back beside the four men and asked, 'What do you mean? You agreed to stay at the station working in exchange for your relatives getting away to sea?'

The party walked on, passing the upraised bar of the level crossing. Dr Cheema and Miss Clairmont were taken aback as they went through a farm gate and walked out into a field where green grass mixed with red weed – a battle for dominance over the pasture. They noted that all seemed to be making for a metal conning tower some distance off. The black of the narrow tower's painted metal was becoming obscured by twisting red weed. Everywhere was the disturbing sight and smell of the Martian freeloading vegetation. The tower seemed to rise out of the soil, and upon getting closer, each realised the upright was attached to the lay of the vast piping system along the flood trench marking the perimeter of the fields. The pipes stretched for a long way, every inch covered by the alien red weed. There was another small conning tower about a half of a mile further along.

Lieutenant Paige sighed. 'There are loads of them and these pipes stretch for miles now. Some of the last ones we took off the train are spares in case we need them. The cattle carts have taken them across the Fens to Friday Bridge. There are store areas for spare piping in scattered locations.'

Miss Clairmont gasped as she peered across the fields of the red Fens. In the distance she could pick out more little red-covered conning towers dotted about. 'Are they all connected to these pipe works?' she asked.

'They are, Miss Clairmont.' Lieutenant Paige smiled.

'Lieutenant Paige,' Dr Cheema protested. 'What has this got to do with Miss Clairmont and I talking with our relatives?'

At that very moment the small conning tower's lid opened, and two more soldiers climbed out. One of the soldiers was another young officer. He immediately called out, 'Please enter the system via that lid, Dr Cheema. We have been expecting you. Beneath is a telephone. Do you know what a telephone is?'

'Yes, I do,' replied the vexed doctor.

Lieutenant Paige smiled and took over. 'There is a line to Wisbech port. Your wife and daughters, plus Miss Clairmont's mother, are on the other end of this telephone line. You can tell them you have been conscripted into the Wake Men medical corps. They'll be put aboard a vessel as soon as you've finished speaking.'

'Well, Wake Men seems to be catching on quick,' muttered Parker.

'You can say that again,' Wickham agreed. 'I only heard it said for the first time back at the station when you brought it up. Now it seems like a regularly used word.'

'The saying has been around for a little while. The requisition man who gave me the freight papers mentioned it to me,' added Mike.

'Well, we've all been kept in the dark on things,' said Parker. 'Kept in the dark and fed on—'

'Not in front of the lady,' hissed Wickham. 'Now we know what it's like to be a mushroom.'

Dr Cheema and Miss Clairmont were shocked. They were conscripted. They realised that by agreeing to serve they could ensure a place for their relatives on board a boat out of the country. In stunned silence, Dr Cheema and Miss Clairmont stepped down from the red and green soil onto the piping layered with red weed that ran along the flood ditches. Then they were directed towards the small conning tower covered in alien vegetation, rising from the iron tank that the piping ran into. First Miss Clairmont climbed up and then down inside the tower. Dr Cheema followed.

There was an awkward silence outside. The soldiers, the railway workers and the admin grasshopper men waited in embarrassed anticipation. They could hear Dr Cheema speaking in Punjabi. Even though they could not understand what was being said, the waiting men recognised the tone – the man was imploring his wife, presumably to take herself and his daughters onto the boat provided.

Then came Miss Clairmont. She began to weep and told her mother that she loved her and would see her soon. It was all very emotional, but she had a duty to the newly formed medical corps of the Wake Men Militia.

When this was finally done, another soldier put his head out of the conning tower and beckoned. They were all to enter the piping system.

Each combatant took it in turns to climb down into the square tank nestled in the flood ditch below ground level. Last to follow were the two grasshopper men. They made off straight down one of the three pipe work openings. Any induction was not for them and they had other things to do.

The pipes connected to the water tank from a three-way flood ditch intersection. The wide observation area was a room. There was a desk upon which were some telephones, plus maps, binoculars and even a rifle rack with weapons stacked, lockers and everything for a small, manned office unit.

'As you can see,' began Lieutenant Paige. 'The observation areas are made of big empty square water tanks, with the circular tunnel piping attached which leads in other directions, towards other sporadic square water tanks that are other observation sectors. You people will be based at a square observation post like this. You can move about by following this piping system. It's lying all along the various fields' many flood ditches.'

The young lieutenant stopped briefly while Miss Clairmont tried to dry her eyes. She had been weeping because of the emotional phone call. Dr Cheema had an arm over her shoulder and tried to comfort her as best he could. He was also emotionally distraught, but deep down the world had become a diabolical place and like the rest, he knew hard decisions had to be made. They were conscripted into a war. A War of the Worlds. Their world had to rely on them, and everything in the world had changed so rapidly – in a matter of hours. It was hard to believe. Yet it was so.

'So now we are medical corps with the new Wake Men army?' Dr Cheema sighed resignedly.

'Yes, Dr Cheema. This is so,' replied Lieutenant Paige.

The conning tower lid was suddenly slammed shut and the last man came down the ladder into the dim gas-lit quarters. The sound of a far-off ventilation system was working. There was a light breeze in the cramped steel room. A wide locker was opened, and some chest waders were pulled out. The new hidden world just commenced without hardly any ceremony.

'We have a rather large pair of chest waders here, Dr Cheema. You must always wear them. There is also a regulatory gas mask that you must always keep upon you. You will notice the small water cylinder against the coal rock beneath the nose filter.'

'Is this an innovation?' asked Miss Clairmont, observing the gas mask that had been given to her.

Paige smiled and nodded. 'It is indeed, Miss Clairmont. We have a workshop further within the pipelines, another tank like this one. Such tanks have been placed all about the complex, not just as observation sections, but ablution areas as well. We have one tank as a workshop. These gas masks are adapted there, for the addition of the small coal pipe attachments going to the filter. Wet coal seems to be effective against the Martian black smoke when mixed with the mask's breathing filter.'

'This is one extraordinary induction, Lieutenant Paige,' replied Dr Cheema.

'Yes, Dr Cheema. I'm afraid it is.' The young officer turned to Miss Clairmont and said, 'There is a screen for you, to put your waders on, Miss Clairmont. Or, if need be, there's an ablution area along the piping.' He pointed to one of the three pipe openings in the square intersection of the tank room. 'It's a little way along there.'

'I'll prefer to use the screen,' she replied. Miss Clairmont was still lamenting her strange conversation using the telephone contraption. For some reason she found the communication apparatus a horrid thing that made people's voices sound crackly and unreal. It was a weird development. New and sterile, like the occurrence of grasshopper men, an appearance coming about from administration staff at her Jesus College and their silly protocol. Now another adopted practice of the breathing mask display. What was it with people, and what were they all turning into?

Quickly, she got changed into the waders behind the small screen – discarding her long skirt and boots, she pulled the chest waders up over her breasts and the straps across her shoulders. On the other side of the screen, the men were also doing the same, within the open square office area – Wickham, Parker and the two rail workers, Bill and Mike. This was to be the new standard wear of the Wake Men Militia. All the headgear remained, but the waders and the gas masks would be worn at all times. Dr Cheema took a little longer to get ready as he got into his larger waders.

'Can I bring my shoes with me?' he asked, holding the items up.

'Of course, Dr Cheema,' replied Lieutenant Paige.

The telephone rang, a low bell sound, answered very quickly by one of the observation soldiers. A staff sergeant. He turned to Lieutenant Paige. 'It's for you, Sir.'

Paige took the telephone and listened to a crackled voice of instructions. Then he replied, 'Very good, Sir. I'll attend the matter immediately.'

The staff sergeant took the telephone and replaced it on the receiver. He seemed to be adapting to the new-fangled device, but it was obvious to the others he wasn't quite comfortable and would need more time to settle with the apparatus.

Paige smiled back at the new arrivals. 'Well then. You are all to be taken to my observation post. It's much like this one, but there is also a small hospital tank close by. There'll be a telephone operator there. You, Corporal Wickham and you, Private…?'

'Private Parker, Sir,' replied Parker.

Again, Paige smiled politely. 'Thank you, Parker. You plus our two adopted rail workers and Dr Cheema along with Miss Clairmont will be stationed at this new observation post. I will escort you all to this place. As I have mentioned, there is another tank in very close proximity to my observation area. Here, there are medical supplies and a few beds for patients when the time comes. Dr Cheema and Miss Clairmont will have both rail assistants for orderlies and assistants of some kind. I'm sure you'll find some use for these men.' He turned to Mike and Bill. 'You chaps will be under the instruction of Dr Cheema and Miss Clairmont. Do you fellows understand?'

'Yes, Sir,' Mike and Bill replied respectfully.

'Top men,' he replied. 'Corporal Wickham, Private Parker. You lads will be lookouts in the observation post's conning tower. I, as your communication officer, and my sergeant, will teach you a few things and you'll learn to liaise with us when the Martians enter our section of the Fenland. Really, you are exchanging the station platform for the underground tank. The new watch is for Martian machine monsters, trains are no longer part of the equation. The job is a more dreadful one, as I'm sure you'll appreciate.'

'Very good, Sir,' Wickham replied.

'Right then, let's not stand on ceremony,' began Lieutenant Paige as he looked at the opening of one of the pipeline tunnels. 'Please follow me.' He crouched down and entered the pipeline.

'Not standing on ceremony is putting it mildly,' added Dr Cheema.

Wickham, Parker, Mike and Bill followed, but Dr Cheema hesitated. He held out a hand for Miss Clairmont to go first. Then he followed her more awkwardly than the rest, because of his tall frame. There were small flickering candles burning inside glass-framed lamps. They were positioned at scattered intervals along the damp piping system. There was also moisture on the walls. It ran down and formed a small tributary, flowing along the bottom of the pipe. A very narrow stream – barely noticeable. Cables ran along the sides of the pipe. All supposed the cables ran the entire length of the pipe works – telephone and telegram wires, no doubt.

Dr Cheema could feel the claustrophobic encroachment of the pipework. It was a very uncomfortable and smothering feeling. He sighed to himself, knowing that somehow, he must adapt to this environment.

They walked for some time in crouched formation and eventually came out by another observation post. Here, two soldiers sat at a desk. One officer and a sergeant. Above, on the ladder section and in the lookout tower, were two more soldiers with binoculars observing the Fens outside through a spy opening. The telephone rang and the officer in charge answered. He held up a hand, instructing Lieutenant Paige and his party to stop.

'Right-ho, Sir. We'll get ready. Thank you.' He put the telephone down and turned to Lieutenant Paige. 'The last train is clear. They are about to blow the raised embankments of the dike wall. The River Nene will spill out into the fields, and the surrounding Fenland will be flooded. I thought you may like to wait here, rather than be in the pipe works when the water hits.'

'Yes, I think that would be best.' He turned to Dr Cheema who was just standing upright after emerging from the pipe tunnel. 'We will wait here while the fen floods, Dr Cheema. We'll let the water settle before we move on. By all accounts this won't take long, the mad inrush of water will quickly settle.'

'Very well, Lieutenant Paige,' replied Dr Cheema.

At the same moment the ground seemed to shake as the *boom* of the explosion ran along the pipework. Miss Clairmont looked at all the men in the underground tank. It was not just her that was frightened, everyone was looking up anxiously, expecting the ceiling to fall in. The telephone rang again, and the officer answered.

'Very good, Sir – thank you.' He put the phone down and turned to everyone. 'Incoming water outside. It's running along the trenches where these pipes are.'

The sergeant looked up the ladder into the lookout tower and called, 'Have you closed and bolted the spy hatch?'

'We have, Serge. Secured and locked,' came the reply.

All felt the sudden incoming rush of cascading water. The intense draught blew past outside of their piped enclosure – a cramped area that was holding. The water was moving further along the outside of the pipe tunnel with an intense rushing sound that slowly abated. All knew the water still flowed, but it was not as extreme. The initial rush was gone as quickly as it came. Now there was the more serene flow of water and the feeling of being submerged.

'This must be what it's like in a submarine,' muttered Parker.

The sergeant looked up again. 'Take a peek, Bruton.'

'Yes, Serge,' Bruton replied and unlocked the small hatch to look outside. 'Blooming heck,' he called from up the ladder. 'It's spreading out over the fields now, Sir.'

'That's splendid, Bruton. It's just what we want. Now we're hidden beneath a grand lake.'

The excitement was infectious. The tunnel system seemed to be working. Parker was looking up and smiling. Wickham looked around at the others and they all seemed relieved and excited by the flood. Even Miss Clairmont smiled to herself as she looked up the ladder, eager for any more shred of information. The atmosphere was suddenly one of grand excitement, but also of a sense of relief and achievement.

'We're under a giant lake! I can't believe it. The whole thing works,' said the other observer soldier.

'Bloody marvellous – what!' exclaimed Lieutenant Paige, clearly approving of the controlled flood.

'I hope the underwater traps will work when we need them, Sir,' added the sergeant to the communications officer.

'I'm sure we'll get to put them to the test,' replied the officer. He looked back and smiled at Lieutenant Paige.

'We'll move on now. I think we're a little eager to get to our little observation post now.' Paige turned and beckoned for his entourage to follow. They all complied and entered the next section of the pipework, knowing they were now below a lake. They could hear and feel the proximity of the water beyond the metal pipework, but it no longer felt enclosing. For some reason they felt hidden and protected. There was the eerie sensation of a chill breeze from the ventilation machines that seemed to be louder now they were submerged.

'How many ventilation machines are there, Sir?' asked Wickham.

'I can't say for sure, Corporal, but there are many circulation units put at intervals all about the various sections of pipe works. Most are by the conning towers with small funnels that can be put into the open, or brought back in when necessary. Did you not notice them at the conning towers?' replied Lieutenant Paige. 'We can shut them down in areas where there is Martian activity. That is a protocol of the entire pipework. An air circulation system can be shut down in immediate proximity of an intruding fighting machine. When it passes, we can restart it. This practice will be used in case the noise of the device alerts the Martian patrols. For there will be patrols, we're certain of this. It may not be heard by the Martians, but Colonel Blake insists on this particular cautionary practice for the time being.'

'That is a sound idea, Lieutenant Paige,' replied Dr Cheema. He was becoming more impressed by the underwater system as he moved uncomfortably along the pipe works.

'They seem to have put a great deal of thought into all of this in a very short space of time,' added Miss Clairmont. 'I can't believe how quickly our world has changed. One moment we're on a train and then in the next instant we're in a vast underwater complex in a completely altered world. It's difficult to take all this in.'

'I understand what you mean, Miss,' replied Wickham. 'I've watched this construction from the railway station for almost a fortnight, but never in my wildest dreams could I have imagined this strange complex.'

Parker muttered sarcastically as all moved along the piping in their uncomfortable crouching gait: 'I bet we get rather sick of the place before long. It doesn't seem as though it was built for comfort.'

'Look on the bright side of things,' said Bill, sniggering.

'I must admit, this is all rather sudden,' whispered Mike in mesmerised awe. 'My old dad used to tell me that a person's life can change on the turn of a groat.'

The entire group made their way along the pipe, feeling more heartened than when they started their journey. Along the way, they came out at other intersections where other observation units were stationed. They all seemed excited and in possession of a new-found confidence. Was it ill placed? Only time would tell.

CHAPTER 4

OBSERVATION POST NINE

'Right, here we are – at last,' said Lieutenant
Paige as he came out of the pipe and into
another huge underwater tank room. The others
following, emerged one by one.

Yet another sergeant was sitting at a small table
with a telegraph machine and a telephone contraption. There were also maps of the surrounding area
with coloured sections of the Fenland labelled A,
B, C and D. These sections were broken down into
ten numbered sections. A familiar funnel extended
from a square box into the narrow conning tower
above the flood line outside. The open box contained a spinning fan that was pointing towards the
next section of piping.

It was then that Corporal Wickham realised
he had seen the same devices at the previous

observation posts, each by the pipe openings. 'Ah, the mist begins to clear,' he muttered to himself.

Dr Cheema stood up beside Wickham and replied, 'Indeed it does, Corporal. Very ingenious for air flow. It does make a loud humming noise that reverberates along the pipe.'

Lieutenant Paige smiled. 'So many things innovated or borrowed from other industries. The whole pipe works are on the spot acquisitions and accommodations from factories all over the Midlands.'

'I can't believe this has been done in mere weeks,' added Miss Clairmont. She was looking at Corporal Wickham, who earlier said he had been observing a miraculous development without fully appreciating the entire thing.

'The freight has been coming backwards and forwards from the yards in March. Day in, day out,' Wickham replied.

'The undertaking must have been enormous,' she added, looking up at the narrow conning tower in wonder.

'This is so, Miss Clairmont,' replied Lieutenant Paige. 'These pipes have been bolted together with added welding flux. This is further sealed with other waterproof pitches. The flood trenches were our guide routes. We also had the knowledge that they would be the first areas flooded when the dike walls were blown. The assembly was quick and straightforward. The ventilation and wiring were what became time-absorbing. We are still laying some sections of cable, but this is almost complete now. These immediate sections, in this area are complete. We can reach our nerve centre via telegram or telephone – a giant web of observation and communication. We can coordinate attacks on Martian trespassers, stay hidden below the water when outnumbered or attack a lone patrol with explosives placed via our underwater swing planks, dropping mines directly in the intruder's path with these swinging devices. We even have trip cables to ring the legs of their machines. We want to fight them with stealth – lure them, then hit swiftly and retreat beneath the flooded Fens.'

Miss Clairmont was visibly impressed. 'Therefore, some of this complex is still work in progress?'

'That's right,' Lieutenant Paige replied politely as he turned to the desk sergeant. 'Been holding the fort, Sergeant Curtis? Splendid stuff, old chap. Here are our personnel for the coming events.' He turned to his entourage of followers and began to make the introductions.

'To all here. Miss Clairmont, Dr Cheema, and others. This is Sergeant Curtis, my liaison and communication sergeant for Observation Post Nine. This is our section, and we will be manning it constantly. You are its staff and just through the pipe here is another tank area for a small field unit hospital – a hospital for this section. As you must be aware, there are other scattered medical rooms all over the pipework. This one by Observation Post Nine will be the work quarters of Dr Cheema and Miss Clairmont, but it's a mere few steps through the next section of pipe. Almost next door.'

'Well,' answered Dr Cheema. 'The Wake Men seem to mean business, Lieutenant Paige. How long did it take to design?'

'It was done on a rudimentary basis, Dr Cheema. We had the notion of laying the pipes in the flood ditches and bolting and sealing the joint sections. We used some mineshaft ventilation systems and began to add things like big empty water tanks for rooms or observation units, and of course small hospitals when the need arises. We've sort of made it up as we went along. Additional ideas followed along the way.'

'But someone must have thought up the concept?' asked Miss Clairmont.

'Colonel Blake had the original idea and others added to the array as we began to bolt it all together. This has been laid out in three weeks. The colonel was on to the plan instantly. He seemed to have a grasp of the opportunity an underwater system may have. We are now Colonel Hereward Blake's Wake Men, and we'll be taking on the Martian fighting machines from these positions – an underwater lair with scattered marshy islands, underwater mines and lassoing traps to hamper the huge machines. We also have use of two fighting machine heat ray weapons, plus some of the strange heat ray hand devices that the creatures use when they emerge from the tripods.'

'How did we get these heat ray cannon things, Sir?' asked Parker in amazement.

Lieutenant Paige smiled. 'There have been a few artillery units that managed to bring down the odd forward patrolling Martian machine. This happened near London and in the surrounding counties. One of them in Cambridgeshire, by a place called Bassingbourn – an isolated tripod craft probing areas before a major assault. On two occasions such weapon captures have been sent to us. We can use these alien weapons on fighting machines that intrude into these flooded Fens if the circumstance is feasible. Hopefully we can bring down these fighting machines, then we cannibalise more weaponry from any Martian tripods that we manage to destroy.'

Dr Cheema frowned. 'Do you think this is possible, Lieutenant Paige. The Martian fighting machines are very formidable.'

'Yes,' agreed Miss Clairmont. 'We saw one when our train pulled out of Cambridge. It was a colossal thing.'

'I know it's a tall order,' said the lieutenant. 'It will not be easy. But the Martian machines can be destroyed when hit, we know that much. These things do have weaknesses. There is a system being worked out to attack the forward patrols and to booby trap the Fens with our underwater mines. This work is already prepared. We can use the lay of this flooded land to our advantage. The entire area is to become a facility of traps for the Martians in their fighting machines.'

Miss Clairmont was astounded. 'So when you bring down a fighting machine, or if you manage to accomplish such a thing, you intend to dismantle the gun things that fire the heat rays?'

'Yes, Miss Clairmont. Hopefully we can try and do something like this once we have manged to bring a fighting machine down, if we manage to achieve such a feat, first and foremost,' answered Lieutenant Paige.

'What about the poisonous vapours and the Martians inside such a machine?' added Dr Cheema. 'These other things would need to be taken into consideration too.'

'Of course, Doctor. That's where the Wake Men units will come into play. They will need to enter the black cloud, for we firmly believe that a downed tripod would saturate itself in black smoke for protection. We know this from previous downed fighting machines. The Wake Men will need to quickly enter the poisonous cloud and engage the Martians in a shoot-out. The creatures will often try to evacuate a machine if they think artillery is going to home in on it. They leave the big heat ray gun upon the appendage when they do this. If they stay put inside the machine and opt to use the more formidable heat ray, then we need to surround it with our own artillery pieces and quickly pound it from different directions, and quickly, before a rescue attempt is made. And there will be rescue attempts by other fighting machines. This is where our own captured heat ray machines can come into play, if it's deemed that we have time to push home an attack.'

'What if you do not have time? It seems very likely that you will not?' Miss Clairmont asked.

'We pull back into the piping and set new mines in the path of a rescuing fighting machine. Options lead to other options,' added Lieutenant Paige enthusiastically. 'If we capture a fighting machine and its gun, we can disassemble the heat ray device and then booby trap the wrecked fighting machine. When another fighting machine comes to retrieve the downed machine, it will also get caught up in the explosive traps that follow an attempted rescue.'

'There is a lot of theory there, Lieutenant,' replied Dr Cheema. 'How much of this has been put into practice?'

'Virtually none of it, Dr Cheema,' answered Lieutenant Paige honestly. 'However, we have a rudimentary notion of what will follow by incidents observed over the weeks, when, on rare occasions, we have managed to bring down the odd fighting machine. The abandonment of machine, the black saturation of poisonous smoke to form a protective "no go" area, plus the retrieving practice of the rescuing Martian fighting machines gives us an idea of the aliens' protocol. Out in the flooded Fens on prepared lands, we can adapt to these anticipated practices with our own improvements. Something the Martians might not be expecting. Use such things to our own advantage, hopefully.'

Dr Cheema gulped. It was obvious that he was not quite as optimistic as the lieutenant. He looked around their submerged tank and deduced that Corporal Wickham and Private Parker were also not so confident, though being subordinate soldiers, they wouldn't dare to say. He then turned back to the young officer and said, '*Hopefully*, being the operative word, Lieutenant?'

'We must always clutch at every straw of hope, Doctor,' replied Lieutenant Paige sincerely. 'It is all we have at the moment. Unless something surer and more substantial can fall into our laps.'

All Miss Clairmont could do was sigh and curse: 'A plague on all Martians.'

'Please let me show you the small hospital tank room. It's just through here,' said Lieutenant Paige.

Miss Clairmont and Dr Cheema followed. Corporal Wickham and Private Parker stayed put, wondering if the sergeant would give them instructions.

Mike and Bill decided to follow on after a moment's pause, each man knowing, in some way, they were to assist Dr Cheema and the lady assistant.

'Should we go up onto the spy hole gantry, Sergeant Curtis?' asked Wickham.

The sergeant looked up from the manual he was scrutinising and gave them a friendly smile. He replied, 'Oh, yes. Might as well get into the swing of things. Take a look at the new flooded Fens.'

First, Wickham ascended the ladder, followed by Parker. There was a narrow gantry big enough for the two men. There were two sets of binoculars as well, sitting on a small shelf. Wickham picked one of the apparatuses up and called down.

'Can we open the spy hole, Serge?'

'Yes,' Curtis replied. 'I know the water level is well below. We have a gauge down here that tells the tidal depth.'

'Does the tide go above the spy hole then, Serge?' asked Parker.

'Not unless there's a freak high tide and that's not very likely,' replied the sergeant.

Wickham and Parker examined the sliding section lid of the spy hole – it was shaped like an oversized letter box. Parker lifted a lock catch as Wickham grinned and slid the door sideways.

Parker gasped as he looked through the slit. There was a vast area of water before them. 'Blinking heck! We're in the middle of a great blooming lake!'

'Look over there,' whispered Wickham. 'There are scattered areas of land. Small marshy islands. Some of them have blokes working on them.'

Parker complied and turned his attention to one of the many small red marshy rises within the great lake. Three soldiers were wrapping parts of an artillery piece in canvas, then carefully concealing them beneath a big clump of alien red weed.

'I think every little marshy island has a field gun,' added Wickham, looking from one small marshy rise to another.

'We have a small island rise just behind us too,' Sergeant Curtis called up. 'If our calculations are correct and it didn't get flooded.'

'What are the soldiers doing on the little islands?' asked Parker.

'Probably wrapping and hiding artillery pieces,' the sergeant answered. He got up from his desk and looked up the ladder. 'Most of our conning towers emerge where the land surveyors said marshy rises would be above the flood water. Each island will have an artillery unit who can go to ground via these conning towers – a short wade into the water to get to a tower. Our artillery unit of three men will be back in soon. They are probably inspecting the disassembled gun pieces and wrapping them in tarpaulin to hide in red weed, the same way as those you are observing. The red weed has a lot of uses, especially when the parasite grows around the conning towers. Helps with concealment in some ways. Open at the slit behind you, you'll see we are just covered by water a few feet from the rise of our own little marshy island of shrubs, trees, and lots of red weed. Our artillery unit will be wading back here as soon as they've packed their disassembled gun away. They may even decide to stay out for a while and get some fresh air. Even if it smells a bit sickly, it's better than staying cramped up in the pipe works. Artillery units do tend to stay above if possible. I should imagine this will be more so now the Fens are flooded and we are properly submerged.'

'I can't believe this,' muttered Wickham. 'They seem to have thought of everything.'

'Well, they seem to have been right so far. Let's hope they're correct about Martian fighting habits too. They haven't been too good on this particular matter so far.'

CHAPTER 5

INSIDE THE HOSPITAL TANK

Lieutenant Paige held his hands out. This was the place. He was looking about the large water tank area they had emerged into from the pipe tunnel.

He smiled at Dr Cheema and Miss Clairmont. 'It seems a little empty now. Maybe it will stay that way. We tend not to have too many wounded. Heat rays can burn a person to the bone within a split second, almost like a ferocious heated acid that devours instantly. The wretched soul doesn't even get to emit a scream, from what I'm told.'

'Yes,' Dr Cheema agreed. 'A wicked form of spontaneous combustion. I've heard this also.' He was looking at the medical equipment and seemed rather focused.

Paige smiled. Apparently, he was encouraged by Dr Cheema's scrutiny. 'There are lots of medical solutions that don't mean a great deal to me. They're in the cabinets over there. I'm sure you people know about such things and their respective uses.'

Miss Clairmont took a deep exasperated breath. 'Lieutenant Paige. You do know that Dr Cheema and I do autopsy work. I assist with the already deceased. Predominately animals. Almost always animals. We also research and study pathogens. Then we tutor the students in this. Sometimes we work on humans, but they are usually mere skeletons that died hundreds of years ago. Some we have worked on died in battle, during the War of the Roses, hundreds of years ago. We don't amputate living people's limbs or make injured living people better.'

'We are more like historians than modern-day doctors, Lieutenant Paige,' agreed Dr Cheema. 'I thought you might want us to dissect a Martian. Do you have a Martian?'

'Oh, my word,' muttered the young officer. 'The blithering grasshopper men told us that you were a doctor and Miss Clairmont was an assistant. I thought a surgeon's assistant.'

'I am a doctor in my specialised field, Lieutenant Paige. And Miss Clairmont is an extremely good lab assistant who went through university and remained as an employee assisting teachers like me. Her expertise beyond being my lab assistant is veterinary pathology. Miss Clairmont is very good with the study of animal blood and bones. Sometimes this is used with human blood and bones within the confines of the university classes.'

Miss Clairmont was equally surprised. 'The grasshopper men are administration staff and internal messengers. They are just "go get" men and they don't understand the versatile differences of the certificate concerning doctorates and in what fields. We suspected that you might want us to examine dead Martians.'

Dr Cheema nodded in agreement. 'I think this sort of thing with wounded and living soldiers will be in a different league.'

'But you know where human parts are, don't you?' asked Lieutenant Paige.

'Well, yes,' agreed Dr Cheema. 'But our subjects are always deceased by the time we get to work on them, as Miss Clairmont said. Sometimes mere skeletons that have been unearthed at archaeological digs.'

Mike and Bill were standing ready to perform assisting duties, but the conversation was going a little above their heads. Secretly each man hoped they wouldn't end up getting wounded. Dr Cheema and Miss Clairmont seemed to display a certain lack of confidence and enthusiasm for healing potentially wounded people.

'Oh dear,' muttered the lieutenant. 'This seems to have been a jinx conscription. I'm afraid you'll have to do the best you can. Maybe get someone else to assist. Then on the other hand, we might get a Martian to dissect.' He looked along the tunnel.

'I doubt if you could drag the thing down here,' added Dr Cheema.

'Well, we must adapt and improvise.' Lieutenant Paige smiled. 'As Colonel Blake of the Wake would no doubt say.'

'Is that one of the colonel's favourite sayings?' Miss Clairmont was looking frustrated and hot.

'Well, perhaps an open-air autopsy would be in order,' suggested Paige.

'Where?' exclaimed Miss Clairmont.

'There is nothing but a vast lake outside,' added Dr Cheema.

'No, Doctor. Most of the conning towers are a short wading distance from the islands in the lake. We have a rise by our observation post, a small mound with a few trees and shrubs, all surrounded by red weed. At least the rise was there before the dike bank was destroyed. Hopefully it still is, or we have lost three artillery men and a field piece,' Paige said, snorting humorously. Then he stopped abruptly as he realised Dr Cheema and Miss Clairmont were not amused.

'I think we are all going to have to move along and take things as they come,' replied Dr Cheema.

'God only knows what that might be,' added Miss Clairmont.

'As a matter of interest, Lieutenant Paige. We would need a strong table on this island mound.' Dr Cheema looked at the four tables in the tank's hospital room. 'We will not get these up through the conning tower. I presume these were put here before the pipe sections were bolted together.'

'This is so, Doctor. But I'm certain we can get something mustered and on standby, if we need such a thing.'

'If you plan to destroy a Martian fighting machine and disassemble the heat ray device for our use, I think it could be feasible that you might come across a Martian inside the contraption,' said Miss Clairmont with a new-found edge of enthusiasm. 'If we are already prepared with a table on this mound or island, and perhaps a tarpaulin covering, it would be a great help.'

'You sound as though you like the idea of dissecting a Martian.' It was Lieutenant Paige's turn to look concerned.

'The prospect of dissecting and learning something is alluring to us, Lieutenant.' Dr Cheema supported his lab assistant's enthusiasm. 'We might be of some help in this way.'

'Oh well, I see.' Paige looked almost embarrassed at the young lady's enthusiasm. He thought it strange and unnatural for a refined-looking young woman. 'Very well then, Dr Cheema. I'll make a phone call to Command Headquarters and tell them of your and Miss Clairmont's field of expertise. Maybe HQ could sort such a thing out with a sturdy outdoor table. Tarpaulin will be easy, and we can hide it all under the robust red weed, use the blithering stuff to our benefit. If you feel this would be to our advantage, of course. After all, we should meet these foul alien beings if we do manage to isolate a fighting machine and bring it down. We do have an approach system for this, and it'll be put into practice rather soon, we hope. Unless the Martians bypass our flooded Fenland.'

'That will be rather unlikely,' said Miss Clairmont, laughing. Her mood was suddenly upbeat. So was Dr Cheema's outlook.

'I say, you two seem as though you're in your happy element at the prospect of carving a Martian up?' Paige could not contain a certain look of disapproval.

Miss Clairmont was equally bemused. 'You soldiers are all for killing one another with guns. Then, suddenly, you decide to get an attack of obscene and strange morality concerning the dissection of these alien beings, Martians that are intent on harming us all, Lieutenant Paige. Why on Earth is this?'

'Referring to Miss Clairmont and I as being in our "happy element" is a rather inadequate way of putting it, Lieutenant Paige,' Dr Cheema remonstrated with an air of good humour. 'We are explorers of dead anatomy, cause of death and so forth. Mainly in animals but also in bones of deceased humans as we have already informed you.'

Lieutenant Paige nodded and smiled. 'I'll leave you people to look around then. As you know, we're only a few yards along the pipe to our Observation Post Nine. Come and go as you please, we don't want to be bogged down with ceremony.' He left and went back through the pipe opening.

In the dim light of the water tank's make-do hospital room, Mike and Bill ventured forward.

'Where does this leave us then, Dr Cheema?' asked Mike.

'Oh, it leaves you chaps in the same situation. I'm certain Miss Clairmont and I will need your help soon.'

'How can you find out things about these creatures by cutting them up?' asked Bill nervously.

'We can learn a great deal Mr...?' began Miss Clairmont.

'Bill Ackerman, Miss Clairmont,' he said removing his rail guard's hat.

'Well, Mr Ackerman, we can learn a great deal by autopsy. An autopsy is what we perform upon a dead body to study its condition. We can learn about cause of death or any unforeseen problems the dead subject might have had in life. Are you with me so far?'

Bill smiled and replied, 'Yes, Miss Clairmont. Will Mike and I be present?'

Dr Cheema answered, 'If you wish to be. We may ask you to get implements or clean them. There will be important things for you chaps to do. Are you up to it? Do you get ill by the sight of blood? I'm told Martian blood is red, just like ours.'

'I'm alright, Doctor,' replied Mike. 'Bill and I have attended accidents on the rails. Not a regular thing but every now and then we've had some unpleasant scenes to deal with along the rails.'

Bill added, 'It comes with the job, Doctor. We've seen a few messy sights in our time. People and animals – especially deer.'

'Splendid! We'll need the use of this experience you have. These unfortunate things will aid us in autopsy,' said Miss Clairmont.

Mike and Bill looked to one another. They grinned nervously then looked back at Miss Clairmont. Each man gulped. Miss Clairmont was a rather pragmatic lady. A direct and to-the-point person.

The tall and imposing frame of Dr Cheema was standing to Miss Clairmont's side and he smiled back at the railmen. Sensing each man's supressed trepidation of the matter, he couldn't help adding his own slice of dark humour. 'You chaps are to be our little brace of peculiar assistant men.'

Lieutenant Paige entered Observation Post Nine and looked up at Corporal Wickham and Private Parker on the gantry. Both men were looking out through the spy holes.

'I'll need to use the telephone, Sergeant Curtis. It seems our doctor and his lady friend are a regular collection of Burke and Hare body-snatcher types. They fancy slicing themselves up a nice fat dead Martian. Seem to think they can learn things by doing so.'

'Ooh!' replied Curtis, twisting his features into a look of disapproval.

'Yes, and our Miss Clairmont is chomping at the bit to go along this line of anatomical exploration.'

'Miss Clairmont seems like she's a real little bundle of joy,' replied Curtis with another distasteful look. 'I wonder about these university types. They do get above themselves. Still, on the other hand, if it's to slice open dead Martians, then let her and Dr Cheema slice away.'

Corporal Wickham called down from the conning tower. 'The Martian war cry is booming away, Sir. There's a big fire beyond the town of March. Lots of smoke too. Not sure, but I think it's further beyond. It might be in Chatteris.'

The lieutenant quickly climbed the gantry ladder and stood by the two soldiers. Parker gave the young officer his binoculars and pointed towards the rising smoke against the red hue. There was the constant *boom* of distant scattered artillery guns and the screeching of alien heat rays. Every now and then the gigantic bellow of a fighting machine's war horn. It sounded like a far-off and unseen giant cow. These noises were not what gripped Paige's attention – it was the vast lake before him. He was inside a narrow conning tower in the middle of this sudden great stretch of water. There was no rushing sound anymore, the water had settled. He had to tear his attention from the sight and concern himself with the sounds of the distant conflict – the War of the Worlds.

'Well, it will not be long now.' Paige sighed. 'They are coming this way and it seems the cacophony of battle is getting louder and closer.' The lieutenant then twisted in the cramped confinement to the spy hole behind, offering a view of the other side of the conning tower. He unlocked and slid open the small hatch. Behind was the small rise of land, a miniature island with shrubs and a couple of small trees. All the Earthly vegetation was covered in the parasitical Martian red weed.

'There are a couple of artillery men on the island, Sir,' said Parker. 'They seem very well concealed. Always wearing their gas masks.'

Paige nodded approvingly. 'I know, Parker. That is good. Gas masks are standard wear outside since the dike was blown. This is now a combat zone, even though the Martians are not here just yet. Our land surveillance people got that right about the islands. Good preparations have been made over the last days. Have you noticed the other little islands here and there?'

'We have, Sir. More of our artillery lads on some of them. All hidden in the red weed,' Parker replied.

'How long do you reckon before the Martian fighting machines get here, Sir?' asked Wickham.

'I think it will be very soon, Corporal Wickham. Very soon, indeed.'

At the same moment the telephone buzzed, and Paige realised he'd been about to call HQ concerning Dr Cheema and Miss Clairmont's need for an outdoor operating table. He looked down as Sergeant Curtis answered the telephone.

'Yes, Sir. I've got that.' He grabbed one of the maps and marked it while listening to further instructions. 'Very good, Sir – will do.' Curtis replaced the receiver and looked up at Lieutenant Paige.

'Was it a report, Sergeant Curtis?'

'It was, Sir. The Martians are destroying some of our Yeomanry units that are dug in at Chatteris. The railway station, the surrounding houses and shops are on fire. The place is being sterilised with black smoke, but this is aiding some of our men in escaping. The new army gas masks seem to be working well. It will not be long before the Martian fighting machines cross the next stretch of fen towards March. The rail yard workers are evacuating into the piping system as we speak and, therefore, the entire town of March is deserted. There's nothing to even try and confront the fighting machines there, Sir. We think the Martians could be here within an hour.'

As quickly as he came up the ladder, Lieutenant Paige was sliding back down. 'The only thing that will slow the Martians down is their own curiosity. Their machines' tentacles will no doubt be exploring the buildings in search of human prey. This often happens when they enter small urban areas. They like to halt and survey their newly conquered territory.'

The telephone rang again and this time the lieutenant picked up the receiver. 'OP Nine, Paige speaking,' he answered.

The young officer listened intently as his eyes widened, looking at Curtis.

'Yes, Sir. I'll be expecting them. Can I ask for a solid table to be brought along with the Wake Men, Sir? Dr Cheema and his aid have requested a sturdy table to put on the mound near the artillery piece, outside. They may have a good use for it. We have tarpaulin here so there's no need for any more of this particular material.' Paige stopped talking and listened to further instructions coming through the telephone earpiece. Clear and precise. A splendid innovation for the pipe system.

'Very good, Sir. We'll be expecting them and thanks for the use of the table, Sir.' He replaced the receiver and turned to Curtis.

'We have Wake Men coming. Our Yeomanry and grasshopper men who will be standing ready at many of the conning towers, including ours. If the fighting machines venture out into the flooded fen, we are to look at opportunities to set off explosives and engage any lone patrols. I think the fight is finally coming to us.'

Up on the gantry platform, looking down, Parker whispered to Wickham, 'This is going to be a real party atmosphere.'

CHAPTER 6

THE WAKE MEN CREATE A HIVE OF ACTIVITY

Dr Cheema and Miss Clairmont were in the observation room, listening to Lieutenant Paige's news. They had been organising medical equipment in their makeshift hospital and now Dr Cheema and Miss Clairmont were ready for their first duty. Each had their gas masks ready, and both shouldered canvas satchels with the Red Cross emblem on the front.

Miss Clairmont perspired in the stuffy atmosphere and she sighed. 'It's been a mere few hours and in that time, our entire world has changed. Even back on the train there was some semblance of normality, but now, down under this man-made lake, the whole world has changed beyond recognition. I keep pinching myself to test if all this is real. Now, here we are with these first-aid satchels and their little red crosses on the side.' Then Miss Clairmont chuckled and added sarcastically, 'I wonder if the Martians will recognise such emblems?'

'I don't think the Martians attended the original Geneva Convention of 1864,' said Dr Cheema. He was nervously trying to lessen the fear that gripped all those inside the observation room.

Lieutenant Paige smiled nervously. 'I doubt they would have taken much notice of it if they had attended, Doctor. From what I've been told, they're rather unsporting chaps.'

'I wonder if we'll be able to tell if they are chaps?' muttered Sergeant Curtis.

Lieutenant Paige gave the sergeant a little nudge with his elbow and nodded towards Miss Clairmont, an acknowledgement of a lady being present.

Miss Clairmont raised her eyes with a look of irritation. It was, after all, a feasible question.

She replied, 'Hopefully, we'll be able to find out if they are gendered as our species is?'

Dr Cheema agreed, it was a practical topic of conversation. 'Maybe like ants or bees?'

Lieutenant Paige raised an inquisitive eyebrow. 'Like a matriarchal female. A group of males and hordes of workers?'

'Who knows? It is very interesting and maybe we can find out,' Dr Cheema replied.

'Do worker ants have no gender then?' asked Paige. He was suddenly interested now the ice had been broken by Miss Clairmont.

Miss Clairmont smiled back. Almost patronisingly, she said, 'In short, yes.'

Sergeant Curtis curiously asked, 'How can you tell what sex an ant is?'

The minor discourse was breaking up the tension, even for Wickham and Parker, who stopped their observation to look down. They had been observing the distant systematic destruction of March town from their position in the conning tower. The fire and mayhem were a few miles away, beyond the flooded area. They had been reporting down to the lieutenant about the circumstance, and phone calls from HQ had been coming in too. The fighting machines were sighted but at distance and above the burning buildings. They looked like silhouettes of enormous gnats on thin legs. It was as Lieutenant Paige had said – the fighting machines were busy exploring the burning debris.

Miss Clairmont smiled at Sergeant Curtis and continued, 'Males are a little smaller than the female ant. A male's head is smaller.' She turned and smiled eloquently at Lieutenant Paige.

'Oh,' he replied. 'Any other things?' The young officer was perplexed now, because of the smile. He realised that Miss Clairmont was not very fond of him and had tried to privately belittle him. It seemed odd that a lady of such intelligence would resort to scoring cheap points.

She added, 'The smaller-headed male ant has longer antennae and wings. Most of the time, you are unlikely to see them, unless you dig into an ants' nest. The most opportune moment when you do get to glimpse lots of male ants would be on a hot day in the summer. I'm sure most might recall when the sky is full of birds who are feasting on these winged ants flying about.'

'I've seen that,' replied Sergeant Curtis.

Miss Clairmont smiled. 'Worker ants are mostly female. They are dependable for the balanced running of an ant colony. Their functions range from caring for the queen and the young, foraging, policing conflicts in the colony, and waste disposal. These workers will most likely never have their own offspring.'

'How can they be female then?' asked Curtis. 'I thought the ant female was unique. I've seen images of them in nature books.'

The conversation was suddenly interrupted by the cacophony of feet moving along the pipe tunnel. All could hear the expected Wake Men entering Dr Cheema's hospital room.

Mike entered OP Nine's area and said, 'There are lots of Wake Men and some grasshopper men.

They're all congregating in your hospital tank, Dr Cheema. There's more of them coming through.'

As Mike entered the large square area a group of Wake Men followed, carrying a solid fold-up table with sturdy fold-up legs. The leading soldier tried to stand upright to salute Lieutenant Paige while holding the table, but Paige quickly put the Yeoman at ease.

'Let's not stand on ceremony in these conditions,' he said with a kindly smile.

The soldier smiled back. 'The table you requested, Sir.'

'Splendid,' replied Paige. 'Please lean the table up against this wall. We'll get it out when our section of Yeomanry goes into the open. How many of you chaps are for Observation Post Nine?'

'A dozen men, Sir. Though there are many more of us who will move on towards OP Eight, Seven and Six, Sir.'

At that very moment, a long line of soldiers wearing their army-issue pith helmets began to pass through in single file. Their gas masks hung loosely about their necks. Here and there, within the passing line, was a grasshopper man in a bowler hat. These individuals wore their gas masks. They looked barely human and more disturbing. Soon the long line of military personnel had passed through their underwater observation tank and disappeared into the next section of tunnel, their foot falls clumping along the pipework in a new discord of retreating sound.

The two soldiers who had carried the fold-up table went with them as an awkward silence descended within the confines of the submerged water tank-cum-office.

It was the other station worker, Bill, who broke the silence. He entered and informed all of the situation back at the hospital tank: 'There are twelve men in the hospital section, Sir. Ten soldiers and two grasshopper men.'

'I see.' Paige frowned and was about to go along the pipe to check the men out.

However, the matter was stopped dead in its tracks. Wickham called down, 'Here they come, Sir.'

Immediately, the telephone rang and Sergeant Curtis picked up the receiver. The NCO acknowledged the instructions being relayed to him while Lieutenant Paige, once again, quickly ascended the ladder to stand on the narrow gantry next to Wickham and Parker.

He was handed the binoculars as Wickham pointed towards the flaming red tinge, rising over the Fens across the lake. It was coming from the direction of March town. There were other distant glows in the surrounding areas – fires from far-off places to the west.

'My word! The fighting machines are flanking us. I doubt if they know or realise it yet, but the Martians seem to have bypassed us on the westward side. I think Peterborough and Whittlesey are in flames.' He leaned across to the other side of the narrow tower where the other spy slit was. It gave a view of the eastern Fens. Beyond the small marshy island, Paige made out further fires with more red haze, glowing a few miles away within the approaching dusk. The far-off sound of artillery and screeching heat rays reverberated from all directions.

'Well, it's been the same for the last hour now. The telephone reports have said as much. But now this new development.' He looked to Wickham, who was pointing towards the March town fires.

Again, Paige raised his binoculars and focused on the huge silhouettes against the background of raging fires and muttered in awe, 'Oh, my word! Here they come – the blighters!'

'I caught glimpses of them, Sir, but I couldn't tell exactly how many there were. I think it's three. One seems extra-large,' whispered Wickham nervously, as though the approaching machine monsters from the burning area around March town might hear him.

Paige agreed. 'I think you are correct concerning numbers. I can clearly make out three black shadows of three fighting machines. They seem to be cautiously striding and stopping to survey the flat fen. They are sweeping the flood with their spotlights. The two front ones look like standard two-pilot Martian constructions, while the one at the rear looks colossal. A four-pilot Martian contraption. A little rarer than the usual machines.'

'Are there none of the smaller one-pilot Martian machines?' asked Parker.

'I haven't made out any small fighting machines,' Paige answered.

Wickham added, 'This darkening dusk brings little in the way of concealment for the Martians, Sir. The horizon in every direction is full of distant infernos and these are lighting up the night sky. Blimey! It's happening everywhere about us. There are more distant silhouettes of fighting machines to the south, west and east. They stand out like sore thumbs, Sir. The firelight makes their positions easy to spot.'

'The Martian front line is sweeping around us and the three from March might bypass us to the side while on the way to Wisbech, the next town in their path, Corporal.'

'What did you make of the one at the rear, Sir? The big thing? It looks like a real piece of work,' Wickham asked nervously, pointing back to the three nearest fighting machines. 'They are still slowly taking one or two giant strides and stopping for a while. Those alien reconnaissance lights keep sweeping the lake area, almost as though they're suspicious of something.'

'They keep stopping to sweep different areas of the lake. They're like a bunch of giant school kids looking for tadpoles,' Parker joked nervously.

Wickham smiled. 'I bet that larger one is the oldest boy in charge of the others. The prefect lad watching from behind.'

Paige acknowledged the Yeoman's observation: 'Yes, Corporal. The larger one is, indeed – a piece of work, as you so expressively put it. I also see what you mean about their cautious approach. Sometimes the lights are concentrated around the scattered island rises above the waterline. But the Martians don't seem to be lingering – nothing is causing them to focus on anything. Our artillery men are well concealed within the red weed. Even the conning towers are wrapped in red weed and they're not attracting undue attention.'

Parker shook his head in disbelief. 'I can't believe this sight! Everywhere out there, in every direction, the night Fens are alive with Martian activity. It makes for a shocking sight! If I hadn't witnessed it with my own eyes, I would never believe it. The Fenland's surrounding horizon – all in flames! Every town and beyond! Our wetlands look like the last place on Earth.'

'Now that the night is here, we can see the panorama because of the fires,' replied Lieutenant Paige. 'That, with the sounds of far-off battles, is hitting home.'

Wickham gasped in dreadful wonder. 'And, in the distance, the far-off fires are lighting up the sky for all to see. We're beneath a vast lake with an orange dome glowing over our position. It's as though we're in Hell. Or, maybe, on another planet? Not Earth's Cambridgeshire Fenland of Great Britain.'

Paige tore himself away from the roaring destruction of distant fires. He focused on the three fighting machines that were slowly making their visual sweeping approach, stopping and starting along the lane towards Ring's End, where the train station had been abandoned during the day. 'I say, that rear machine does continue to look awfully big, Wickham. I wish we had further information on such a blighter. It looks a little on the special side where Martian fighting machines are concerned.'

'It'll look even bigger when it gets up close, Sir,' Parker muttered in awe.

'Yes, thank you for that tantalising slice of insight, young Parker. We just need more certain information about it. Have any of you chaps come across such sightings or been given information from passing bulletins? I know such guides are circulating. I've never found time to sit down a read the perishing things.'

'I have. There is a small pamphlet manual on the shelf here.' Wickham picked up the booklet.

Paige frowned as he read the cover in Wickham's hand. '*Know Your Martian Fighting Machine* by Colonel H. E. Blake!'

Wickham smiled. 'Yes, Sir. It's not a bad read, with some splendid diagrams. I've been looking through it at the various drawings. I wouldn't like to be the fellow who had to get close and sketch these blighters, that's for sure. It reports that big bloke machine as being crewed by four Martians. It says, "not as numerous as the two or one-crew machines", but it is certainly very imposing to the eye.'

'As though the others aren't?' replied Paige with a tone of irony. 'Splendid. Armed with such knowledge, our Martians will quake on their huge unwieldy legs.'

'Why wish they wouldn't keep stopping?' asked Parker. 'Their huge torch things keep moving about the flooded fields. I want them to keep moving and walk on past.'

Wickham gulped as his eyes once again scanned the fiery horizon. 'The whole surrounding area is complete bedlam, and we are able to watch it all from here. It feels safe here, but for how long?'

The telephone rang again, and they could hear Sergeant Curtis answering and responding to instructions. He put the telephone back down and called up to the gantry to Lieutenant Paige.

'Sir, we are going to try and lure those three fighting machines into the flooded area. Colonel Blake wants to engage them in combat!'

'Oh, bloody Hell!' the lieutenant said, allowing himself a brief call of exasperation, and then quickly pulled himself together. 'Are they going for the unmanned island lure with fireworks?' asked Paige.

'Yes, Sir. But they will not set off the firework bait until the fighting machines are in the right place to walk one of our better booby-trap approach paths. The Martians need to get a little closer to the station area before we try to lure them along one of our best prepared approaches. The underwater mines are being swung into place as we speak and there are also huge explosives buried along the way towards the chosen island. There are many hidden explosives in the flooded fields – we can detonate when the fighting machines are over or by them.'

Lieutenant Paige sighed. He never thought they would engage against such odds, especially on a first-time attempt. 'Does top brass know there are three?'

'They do, Sir. But most seem to think only the two smaller ones will investigate. According to most practices in the field of Martian deployment, the bigger ones come in when there is a problem of continued resistance. If the bigger, third one does accompany the two-piloted machines, we'll just let the mines do the work and stay hidden. But top brass seems to think the larger fighting machine might move on towards Wisbech. It'll return if the others don't reappear. I think the colonel seems to be banking on this happening.'

'I wonder if the colonel wrote a pamphlet on that one?' Paige muttered to himself. Wickham and Parker heard but the others below did not.

CHAPTER 7

PUTTING THE MARTIANS
TO THE TEST

Paige handed the binoculars back to Corporal Wickham. Outside, the world was going mad. The three Martian fighting machines were still moving along the rise of the railway embankment, stopping and sweeping areas with light, then taking two or three strides to repeat the process over the new man-made lake.

'Keep your eyes peeled for anything that might develop, Corporal Wickham,' said Paige.

'Yes, Sir,' replied Wickham and put the binoculars to his eyes.

The lieutenant thought everyone inside the piping system must be insane, including himself as he took a deep breath. Just below the observation gantry was the confined area where frightened personnel waited with growing concern. Perhaps, like Paige, they wondered if the Wake Men would venture outside and confront the Martians? Or was it just fantasy talk and grand posturing?

As Paige turned to descend the gantry's narrow ladder, he could feel the new and more dreadful atmosphere, a sweating fear that was growing among all the waiting people. At the bottom, he took note of their faces. He tried to smile at them reassuringly but it didn't seem to work. There were just the continuous silent and frightened looks that said it all. Each expression glistened with dripping sweat, a collective front of pure fear – an anxiety that each individual was silently fighting to overcome.

He could not help but observe Miss Clairmont, looking up towards the conning tower gantry, aware that outside, diabolical and horrendous events were unfolding. She was trying to contain her anxiety with a resolute folded-arm stance. The lieutenant wanted to try and say something reassuring, but decided Miss Clairmont might not appreciate such special attention.

'Why does Colonel Blake think this big fighting machine will not respond to the bait, Lieutenant Paige?' Dr Cheema asked. The man was very concerned and like everyone else in the observation post, he was not confident of such preconceived notions.

'Our forces have been filing reports of method and strategy concerning Martian fighting machine activity, Dr Cheema. And the supposition of *might* is a little loose, in my personal opinion. I suspect it is in yours, too. But even if the larger fighting machine does come, I think the colonel would be pleased. His ambition is to destroy such a colossal machine. He also wants to try and capture a machine to use against the Martians. The underwater pendulum systems can swing out from various hidden locations – they're worked from outside. These slide mines can move up and along the swinging planks and can be detonated by a fighting machine's legs. I believe these can and will work.'

'Surely that would be extremely dangerous?' exclaimed Miss Clairmont nervously.

There was a brief silence in the tank as all the men looked to Miss Clairmont. Lieutenant Paige's previous sympathy vanished. The officer's face beamed with twisted glee and he decided to indulge himself with a flippant reply. After all, Paige felt he owed the young lady a return remark on the patronising front. He raised an eyebrow as his thin moustache twisted into a delighted grin. 'Yes, it is rather dangerous. Thank you for that inciteful observation, Miss Clairmont.'

Miss Clairmont raised an angry eyebrow. She wanted to retort but couldn't think of anything to say. Instead, she just looked embarrassingly flummoxed.

Paige turned to Curtis and added, 'I'm going to bring the Wake Men through. There is a strong possibility that we'll be hazarding this outside menace on an up-close basis once our explosives start going off.'

The lieutenant then ducked into the pipe and made his way towards the unused hospital tank where his ten Wake Men and two grasshopper men awaited instructions.

Miss Clairmont looked vexed, and indulged the notion of pursuing the officer, but Dr Cheema gently held her arm. 'Miss Clairmont,' he whispered. 'Please do not do what I think you are about to do?'

'Well... I thought he was being very sarcastic,' she hissed under her breath.

'When we're alone in the hospital, I would greatly appreciate a quiet word with you. And I humbly ask you not to get into an argument with Lieutenant Paige at this time, Miss Clairmont. It would be rather inappropriate, especially under the present circumstances.'

Miss Clairmont took a deep breath and contained her irritation. Dr Cheema was a man she respected, and he seemed concerned. She would comply with his well-intentioned advice.

'Fighting machines are moving forward again,' Wickham called down from his platform as he watched through the conning tower porthole. 'Approaching Ring's End railway station. They are continuing to be orderly. They stop and sweep their search beams over the flood area and then move a little closer before stopping for another sweep.'

Sergeant Curtis began to send the news via the telegraph. He was instructed to use the telephone for incoming information when events were getting hectic. No sooner had he finished the telegram, he got a return telephone call. He picked up the receiver and listened to further instructions and replied, 'Yes, Sir, will do.' He put the receiver down and turned to Mike, the seconded rail worker. 'Could you please request Lieutenant Paige to return with his Wake Men detachment. I think they are getting ready for the big one.'

'Will do, Sir,' Mike replied.

'And it's not Sir. It's Sergeant.' Curtis smiled at the civilian worker.

'Sorry, Sergeant,' he called back as he made off along the piping.

Within moments the station worker was back and suddenly soldiers entered the observation post. They packed the entire little square area. Dr Cheema, Miss Clairmont, Mike and Bill were squashed up against the cold metal wall of the tank, watching the influx of troops forming two lines. Some looked about the confined area with mixed apprehension and willingness. When the command came, they would bravely put their gas masks on, climb the ladder and venture out into the open. Only the bowler-hatted grasshopper men, from the university, were already wearing their gas masks. Their rasping breath through the front air filter filled the room with an enhanced eerie aura, their wide circular dark lenses completing their scary aspect as though each bowler-hatted being had metamorphosised into a giant hideous insect.

Dr Cheema whispered to his group, 'Hopefully, a Martian will be disturbed by such a sight too.'

'I certainly hope so,' Miss Clairmont whispered back.

Finally, Lieutenant Paige returned through the pipe opening and pushed his way through the throng of gathered soldiers. Rifles were held upright and ready and with bayonets fixed.

'Are the ventilation pumps working alright, Sergeant?'

'They are, Sir.' The sergeant looked at the filter boxes and flumes above each tunnel opening on either side of the submerged tank. 'That's the whirring racket we can hear.'

'Yes, of course,' Paige replied. 'It's funny how one can dismiss certain humming sounds of machinery when it is constantly going.'

Miss Clairmont's nose wrinkled at the smell of sweat and tobacco. She noticed that many of the soldiers' khaki pith helmets were stained with greasy residue. No doubt from condensation on the inner iron of the pipe network where travel required people to be bent double while moving. Even the brown strap across the front of the pith helmet looked grubby. It was to be expected and she was sure such minor things would be less noticeable in the coming dreadful future. The army was about to engage the Martian fighting machines. Up until now, the army had won scant success, but these soldiers were still going to try. They were frightened, all could see that, but they would try anyway.

Soon the damp atmosphere began to get stuffier. It was better than being cold, but still the discomfort grew. The anxiety of waiting beneath water in a claustrophobic water tank tested everyone's willpower. They fed off one another to remain silent. Outside, the colossal alien fighting machines would be striding around the lake in search of humans.

Once again, the telephone rang and Curtis picked up the receiver.

'Yes, Sir,' he replied into the contraption and nodded to Lieutenant Paige. 'Preparations are in place, Sir. Action is about to begin.'

'Splendid, Sergeant. Let's get ready for our Martian foes.' Paige quickly climbed back up to the gantry and was beside his two-man observation crew. 'I bet you chaps wish you were back on the train platform getting bored out of your wits?' he joked light-heartedly.

Wickham and Parker quietly chuckled through the dreadful expectation of their fear-enhanced thoughts.

'They've stopped again. This time at the station, Sir.' Wickham pointed towards the building beneath the orange-tinted night sky. 'There are two of the average-sized double-crewed tripod machines. They aren't half glowing under that weird fiery sky, Sir.'

'Indeed they are, Wickham. But look at that enormous four-crew bounder of a machine behind them,' replied Paige in awe.

Parker gasped as he peered through the observation slit. 'It's standing further back, yet it blooming dwarfs each of the front machines. Why did you not mention that one first, Corp?'

'I wanted to save the best bit until last, but you've just nicked me punchline, Parker.' Wickham was trying to be humorous.

Paige sighed fearfully as he looked at the gigantic fighting machines from Mars. 'Look at them! The whole burning world is their stage.'

'While the sounds of far-off battles are the wicked machines' evil orchestra,' added Wickham.

'Well, my trusted thespian critic,' Paige chuckled nervously, 'we have one of the best seating areas in the theatre.'

'A royal balcony, Sir,' said Wickham, laughing.

'With all the best lime lighting to boot,' added Parker, trying to keep in with the banter. It helped steady their tested nerves.

Curtis slammed the telephone down again and called up, 'Fireworks are set! Pendulum mines, getting ready, Sir.'

'Excellent, Sergeant Curtis,' Paige replied. Then he added with a tone of humorous understatement, 'Well, chaps, I think things are about to liven up a tad.'

At the same moment, a small island rise that was just a few hundred yards away from their Observation Post Nine spy tower began to crackle and bang with a cascade of fireworks. The sparkling flashes were the decoy. The quick array of fireworks abruptly stopped as quickly as they began.

'A small exercise in attention-seeking,' whispered Paige as he raised his binoculars.

'It's worked!' hissed Wickham.

Further away, beyond the lake, by the vicinity of the distant train station, one of the forward Martian tripods raised a twisting tentacle. It was wrapped about the long pole-shaped heat ray device. There stood the battle-ready fighting machine. All focused their attention upon the demonic effigy framed against the hellish landscape.

'I think that blighter is about to fire its heat ray,' whispered Paige.

A terrifying chill settled as the heat ray's whirring system started. A split-second warning ahead of the ear-splitting screech and the blazing bolt of light – the glowing blue energy that shot across the lake to hit the island of fireworks. An impressive explosion erupted. Fire and earth lifted high and out into the surrounding lake. Everywhere, splashing debris and all about Observation Post Nine's little red weed-covered conning tower.

'Oh, my word!' muttered Wickham with a tone of dread. 'That seems to be something of a reply.'

'That's grabbed the chap's attention. But the next bit is going to be a little trickier,' hissed Paige, trying to contain the tension building inside his stomach.

'If it works, Sir?' replied Parker fearfully as he watched the two standard fighting machines advance.

'The two small ones are approaching,' added Wickham excitedly.

'And the taller one is turning!' exclaimed Paige, suddenly clutching at an opportunity of enthusiasm. 'My word, I think HQ were right. The big blighter's going towards Wisbech!'

All watched in wonder as the biggest titanic fighting machine turned away from the firework show. It began to stride away in the direction of Wisbech, uninterested in the attention-seeking event. The two standard-sized machines were equipped to deal with the conundrum of firework island.

Parker gulped and then added with anxious humour, 'Well, it is rather nice there in the summer, Sir. No disrespect to Wisbech, but that place is welcome to the blooming thing.'

Lieutenant Paige chuckled and whispered, 'I doubt the Martians will receive a welcoming committee, Parker. Hopefully the last civilians are on the boats going out into the Wash. Please mention nothing of the taller machine's direction to Dr Cheema and Miss Clairmont. It will cause added concern to an already delicate situation.'

Parker looked down from the raised platform to the waiting Wake Men. All of them, packed in the tank area and eagerly wanting to climb the ladder. His gaze also settled upon Dr Cheema, Miss Clairmont and the two rail workers, squashed against the iron wall behind the soldiers.

'We've got a nice group of people standing ready,' said Wickham. 'But I don't think they can do anything useful with the weapons at hand.'

A surprise muffled explosion came from outside. It was not Martian. It was man-made. Parker and Wickham could tell by the detonation's resonance.

'That's one of ours!' Parker exclaimed.

All three soldiers quickly returned their attention through the viewer slit. Of the two approaching fighting machines, the rear tripod had abruptly stopped. A plume of water had risen next to one of its three legs – an unimpressive little eruption of water that had gone off by the alien contraption's leg. The ignition seemed half-hearted – a slightly puny affair.

'Not the obliging explosive roar I was expecting,' Parker muttered.

'Just a small boom with a minor fountain of water lifting unimpressively to the side of the fighting machine's leg,' agreed Wickham.

'With all the Martian weaponry showing off its might, our little reply does seem dashed unconvincing,' muttered Paige with a twinge of disappointment.

'However,' continued Wickham with excitement. 'On second thoughts, I think it was a hit, Sir.'

'With a pendulum mine?' Parker asked.

Below, the telephone rang, and Curtis was his usual quick self in answering. He put the receiver back and called up, 'OP Seven hit one with a pendulum-strapped mine, Sir!'

'Is that what it was,' he called back, and added cynically, 'I thought someone had thrown a brick and caused a splash beside it.'

'Ah, I don't know though, Sir!' Wickham was pointing at the observation slit. 'I think that fighting machine is in a spot of bother.'

'Something is bothering the blooming thing,' added Parker delightedly.

'Good Lord!' muttered Paige with new-found hope. 'Something is wrong with its leg. The blighter is wobbling!'

Nervously, Paige turned his binoculars to the receding back of the larger fighting machine that was striding away towards the market town of Wisbech.

'That bigger machine is still moving away. It's taken no notice. Thankfully, it's not returning.'

'Neither is the leading fighting machine approaching firework mound,' added Wickham encouragingly. 'It's cautiously approaching the island and seems unaware of its companion's dilemma.'

'Well, the lead machine's ignorance is our little slice of bliss,' joked Paige.

Suddenly, there was a second muffled *boom* by the already stricken fighting machine. Again, it caught the men by surprise. Another small geyser of water lifted to the side of the machine's other leg.

Parker muttered, 'It's almost half-hearted, compared to the type of explosions we've witnessed from distant battles close to the horizon.'

'Yet, there was a sense of devious harm,' added Paige enthusiastically.

'A point scored,' agreed Wickham as he watched with new-found and devoted delight.

'Another pendulum mine, no doubt?' Paige looked down from the gantry to his sergeant seated at the table. The trusted NCO was waiting eagerly for the telephone to ring. It did and everyone inside the observation tank was feeling excited by the unfolding reports of the commotion outside. The observation crew's banter had informed them all of events in the waiting silence. Even whispers could be clearly heard. The mood was captivating.

Attention was turned to Curtis on the telephone. The sergeant gulped as his eyes lit up with excited surprise. He answered enthusiastically, 'Yes, Sir. Our observation crew just witnessed the second explosion. Very good, Sir. Very good indeed. Will do, Sir!' He put the telephone back and looked up with wide-eyed delight. He took a deep breath and then continued, 'Observation Post Ten, Sir!'

'Yes, Sergeant Curtis, don't keep us in the dark.' It was an amused quip from Paige.

'OP Ten have the firework island loaded with explosives. The whole blooming place is planted with dynamite. They're going to detonate it when the lead fighting machine starts its survey of the place. They've got enough stuff to blow the thing back to Mars, Sir.'

Among the waiting Wake Men and the medical crew were gasps of wicked joy.

For the observers on the gantry, attention was, once again, diverted to the stricken fighting machine. A warning bellow was emitted from the giant contraption. It was teetering as though struggling for balance. Then, to add to the already excited mood, a third *boom* erupted close to the other of its three legs.

'Another pendulum mine!' hissed Parker through gritted teeth as he gratifyingly held up a clenched fist.

On this occasion, the exploding jet of water rose a little higher, almost as though offering the observation crew a slice of extra fulfilment. All three gulped as the entire machine teetered back and forth. For a dreadful breath-taking moment, each observer thought the fighting machine would recover. The tension was almost unbearable. Alas, to the delight of the mesmerised observers, the vile edifice slowly toppled forward. The enormous alien creation gathered speed as it plunged into the man-made lake, the upper body casing hitting the water with a colossal impact around ten yards from the observation tower. A huge splash as an exploding stream of cascading lake water hit the turret. A deluge of water forced its way through the rectangular spy slit. It rained down upon the waiting and disciplined Wake Men who were standing with rifles and bayonets held upright.

This brief downpour was followed by a high, rolling wave and an undercurrent of force – a secondary and more palpable hit upon the conning tower. The observation slits were slammed shut, but the waiting Wake Men, standing below, staggered as the force of moving water hit the tank. Thankfully, the pipes and the tank held firm, and all regained their balance.

When the shock wave passed, Lieutenant Paige slid the observation lid back open. The stricken fighting machine's half-immersed trunk was very close. All about the wrecked mechanical demon was a bubbling effervescence. The entire spectacle was surreal. The orange-tinted night sky and the glow on the disturbed lake water – it was as though they were on another planet. Not Earth – not Britain. Some dreamlike, unrecognisable nightmare world.

'Oh, my word! This blighter is well and truly ours,' roared Lieutenant Paige, the sweat of fear and excitement making for heightened glee.

'The lead fighting machine! It's stopped!' yelled Parker in alarm. 'I think it's going to the walloped Martians' aid!'

'I think you're right!' added Wickham in panic.

Nervous shuffling and murmuring came from the Wake Men below. They were itching to get outside. They had moved beyond the discomfort and dread of their cramped conditions. Now their circumstance was almost demanding to be allowed outside, even among the vile blood-sucking Martians. Anything to be out of the enclosure.

The three observers were oblivious to the telephone ringing as they watched the lead tripod. The mechanical alien monster had reached the marshy island. It had bent slightly forward. The huge vehicle's Martian operators had started the reconnaissance of the strange mound where fireworks had been exploding. Three of the giant's tentacles were in the process of exploring the mixture of vegetation – the Martian red weed and Earth's green foliage, battling for dominance of the marshy landscape beneath the strange, flaming night sky.

Then slowly, the unexpected collapse of its companion brought the lead machine to a faltering halt of duty.

'At last,' hissed Parker.

Lieutenant Paige sighed. 'The stricken structure's monumental collapse into the lake has finally diverted the lead machine's attention.'

'Yes,' Wickham agreed. 'Midway into the lead machine's investigative exercise, Sir.'

'And not a moment too soon,' Parker added.

Paige muttered keenly, 'This is so – the Martian crew in the lead machine finally have their interest captured.'

Wickham was equally captivated by the new development and said excitedly, 'Our hit on the following alien machine was a rather sound attack, Sir. Better than we initially expected.'

'And something completely unexpected for the leading alien machine crew, I would wager.' Paige completed the speculation.

The observing soldiers were suddenly jolted out of their hardened awe. The deep *boom* of a field gun!

Instantly, the off-white understructure below the green visor screen of the Martians' machine cabin clanged. A small puncture hole suddenly appeared, surrounded by a minor puff of smoke. An artillery shell had smashed through the curved hull. For a split second all were astounded by the appearance of the projectile's immediate visual damage, but then the small structural impairment was thrown away into an unimpressive perspective. A split second later, the transparent green resin of the oval view port ruptured and blew outwards – the result of a confined explosion within. An explosive force, needing release. A massive outburst of disgusting green secretion escaped from the confining screen membrane, followed by an inferno of ballooning flame, the vile green wreckage and flame spraying over the marshy island.

'Blooming Hell!' gasped Parker. 'Greener than the perishing red weed.'

'Martian green doesn't count,' replied Wickham, flippantly trying to act brave.

'That was a splendid shot,' called Paige.

'I think it was fired from the artillery crew on the island behind,' yelled Wickham.

Paige turned in excitement and looked out of the east view spy hole. He saw the artillery men of Observation Post Nine's little marsh island rise. The three-man artillery crew had taken it upon themselves to quickly assemble their field gun and take a close-quarter shot. They were very well concealed by the parasitical red weed but the smoking gun barrel alerted Paige to their position.

It also alerted the shell-damaged fighting machine. The mechanical monster let out a huge and deep bellow. Its fiendish yell fanned out across the marshy Fenlands under the night's polluted orange sky. It was hard to know if it was a war cry or a distress call.

'Oh, my blooming Gawd! That thing can probably still stand,' said Parker, terrified by the sight.

'Even after our blokes put a shell straight into it,' added Wickham, equally as frightened.

'Surely the Martians inside must be injured?' added Parker.

Paige replied, 'Injured, maybe? But is that enough, old boy?'

For a fleeting moment, each observer drank in the dreadful sight. Some of the fighting machine's appendages remained extended within the island's foliage. The observation unit gasped again as the new drama unfolded before their awestruck eyes. The forward arched mechanical titan, with its destroyed and smoking view port, slowly withdrew its exploring tentacles – a task no longer required.

As though contemplating the insult of the strike, the outlandish mechanism menacingly began to straighten its long folded legs, each limb groaning as the protesting joints of the monstrosity began to align, the inner smoking cabin rising above and before the fiery panorama.

Again, all inhaled with perspiring fear at the sight of the elevated smoking Martian control room, each observer trying to catch a glimpse of the vile aliens that were still able to operate their battered vehicle. Green gunge streamed down the front of the weathered off-white cabin. Below, a thin stream of grey smoke still spewed out, where the shell hole appeared. It all made for a breath-taking sight.

'It looks like a giant ugly face with a big spot on its chin,' Parker mumbled.

Wickham gulped and then whispered, 'I once knocked a good boxer down. I remember him standing back up with that type of posture.'

Parker replied nervously, 'What, before the count ended? With a "now it's my turn look"?'

'Yep,' replied Wickham, transfixed by the sight.

'What happened?' Parker was also gripped by the astounding sight.

'I got my lights punched out,' Wickham replied.

Paige swallowed and pointed to the machine's downward bearing and the ruptured green oval screen. 'Look!'

At such a short distance from the lookout slit, the ghastly persona of the injured mechanism was clear. A towering, enormous structure, like a demonic sentinel enhanced by the far-off hue of the surrounding horizon's front-line battles. The forward-facing capsule's bent down position appeared contemptuous as it scanned for the feeble human assailants who had dared to strike it.

Within the fighting machine's shattered opening, the inner radiance provided for a further chilling and abhorrent sight. Each soldier made out an organic and slimy-looking appendage, slithering over a control panel. At the end of the flexible limb were three thin, miniature tentacles. They operated various appliances with effective dexterity.

Parker whispered fearfully with his innocent and secular comparison, 'I saw an octopus in a zoo, once. The thing was inside a huge glass tank. It had tentacle arms just like that.'

'They are either arms or tentacles,' Wickham corrected without malice. It was just a whim – something to nervously add.

Parker accepted Wickham's amendment and added, 'Oh, yes. And without those three little, tiny tentacles at the end, which these Martians seem to have. The digits that look like, but are not, fingers.'

'Well, yes. But they certainly act like fingers,' Wickham admitted.

Parker looked at the corporal and raised an eyebrow. He felt that whatever opinion he might offer, Wickham would find a way to greet it with an opposite point of view. But Parker was the lowest-ranked soldier and decided it wasn't prudent to say anything in front of Lieutenant Paige.

'It's operating some sort of control,' muttered Lieutenant Paige. His morbid fascination aligned with that of his two subordinates.

At the same instant one of the outside mechanical tentacles began to rise. It was holding the long heat ray apparatus and was pointing down – a trajectory that suggested the artillery men and their field gun were the target.

Curtis called up after slamming the telephone down. 'Close ports, Sir! The second one is about to be blown to kingdom come!'

Wickham complied with the west view port while Paige shouted to the artillery men through the east view. 'Take cover!' he screamed through the observation opening and then banged it shut.

The start of the alien whirr from the fighting machine's device was heard briefly within the observation tank. It was barely a split second before being fiercely drowned out. The Martian weapon never reached the crescendo whereby the heat ray would have been released. A bigger man-made explosion happened!

Once again, the pipe system shook violently to the colossal roar outside. Paige stretched forward and managed to grab Parker. The young soldier had stumbled back from the force and almost fell off the platform.

'Hold tight there, Parker. Those chaps down there have raised bayonets,' said Paige.

'Thanks, Sir.' Parker gulped as he looked below at the long wicked upright blades upon the staggering Wake Men's rifles.

'Blooming heck, Parker. You could have been skewered like a pig,' said Wickham.

'It means nothing to us. Absolutely nothing, does it?' Parker replied, gripping the handrails while the pipe system was still shaking.

'What do you mean, Parker?' Lieutenant Paige asked, grabbing the rails too.

'We are indifferent about skewering pigs. But knowing the Martians think of us in the same way – food or meat to be eaten – we are like pigs fighting for survival.'

Paige nodded and accepted that the young soldier had a point. 'Against an indifferent enemy that treats us as a food source by sucking us dry of our blood.'

'Yes, Sir,' Parker shouted above the cacophony of external clamour.

Outside, debris was falling and splashing into the flood. The shaking had stopped but the cascade of earth and rubble was making itself known.

Paige looked at the young soldier. 'Well, pigs don't have the capacity to fight back as we do, Parker. If a pig could, I'm certain it would find ways of preventing its horrid end. Even if it meant destroying us human predators.'

Below the gantry and among the staggering Wake Men, Paige made out Dr Cheema and Miss Clairmont. Each clutched a wall rail, wearing looks of terror. Gradually, the fear subsided from their faces. Before them, the soldier contingent began to straighten up.

'I'm surprised the pipes have held,' Wickham garbled nervously.

'I am too,' Paige replied. 'The system seems a lot sturdier than I presumed.'

The submerged complex was still reverberating from lesser shock waves. But the worst was over. All those within had expected to see the inrush of water from somewhere, maybe a rupture by the walled rivets. But no! Amazingly the piping held. Now just nominal fear etched faces, eyes scanning everywhere about the submerged tank and piping system. Surely a breach would happen somewhere amid the shaking structure?

'How the Hell we are all still in one piece is beyond me,' called Parker, still gripping the gantry rail for dear life.

Wickham called down to Curtis, 'Can we take a look, Sergeant? I think the worst is over. There are no more explosives to be set off, are there?'

Everyone was calming down from the ordeal. The Wake Men looked even more anxious in the dim lighting of the huge tank area, shadows and bayonets of soldiers wanting to be free of their circumstance.

'Yes, I think a quick look would be in order, Corporal,' he called back.

Slowly and with dread, Paige slid the western view lid open. His eyes widened with astonishment to the sight before him. Like the first downed fighting machine, they were greeted by the spectacle of a second destroyed Martian vehicle. The entire structure was lying away from the earth-wrecked firework island, forced as such by the power of the explosion. It was partially submerged in the lake and not far from its other destroyed fighting machine companion.

'Blooming Hell!' Wickham responded. 'The entire thing must have been lifted and thrown away from the mound when it blew up. It's lying a little way away from all that churned-up earth.'

Once again the telephone rang, and Curtis answered. It was followed by the usual replies of compliance and then replaced. The sergeant looked up to the gantry observer crew again and said, 'One of our captured heat ray devices is in place by Observation Post Eight, Sir. They have clear sightings of each damaged machine's heat ray weapons. Also, a clear line of fire. They will fire two shots. The sweeping lighthouse method. Something spoken of in those theory talks, Sir. Each one will hopefully sever the protruding devices from the tentacles that hold the weapons. When these fall into the mud or water, our two grasshopper men will wade out and place flag markers. The Wake Men will assemble outside, on the shallow flood of the gantry awaiting the order to advance. But only when heat ray devices have been severed.'

Paige looked down and called, 'Right, both grasshopper men come aloft. Wake Men stand ready. Theory is about to be tested in practice.'

A Wake Men corporal repeated Paige's instructions: 'Grasshopper men climb the ladder. Wake Men stand ready. Theory is about to be put into practice.'

Wickham looked to his friend Parker and raised his eyes upwards. He wanted to say something like, 'There goes a jobsworth,' but managed to contain it to his exasperated look.

Parker raised an amused eyebrow and smiled. The Wake Men corporal seemed to enjoy barking out orders and had a conviction of his Wake Men leadership.

The narrow iron ladder began to quiver as the two grasshopper men ascended with their gentlemen's bowler hats, looking up through the eerie dark lenses of their creepy gas masks. They moved like stalking predatory insects with holstered handguns on their chests, below their narrow-ribbed breathing apparatus.

Lieutenant Paige's attention was focused outside. As the officer in charge of the post, he wanted to see the Wake Men's captured heat ray at work. He noticed the first stricken machine's main outer weapon through the hissing steam rising about the partially submerged contraption. The threatening weapon was held upright, in the grip of a mechanical feeler, moving about in a menacing manner, as though searching for a target from its downed position. It was difficult to tell, but Paige knew, or felt, the Martians were still inside, operating their wrecked machine, still able to function in besieged and desperate circumstances.

'The Martians still seem ready with their big heat ray guns, Sir,' said Parker.

'Yes, Parker. I don't think the blighters are going to give up without further fighting,' agreed Paige.

The two grasshopper men reached the gantry. Wickham noticed the long thin metal stakes with small orange triangular flags – the markers for the next part of their task.

A whirring sound, from outside, hissed. It was beyond the scene of their brief battle, further along the underwater pipework at Observation Post Eight.

'That's our heat ray device,' Paige murmured with enthusiasm.

The whirr lasted a moment as it reached a higher crescendo. A bolt of blue glowing energy shot out and swept over the lake, a small arc spreading like the beam of a light tower sweeping across the sea. The captured alien beam scythed through the first wrecked tripod's appendage – the very feeler holding the heat ray device. The entire apparatus toppled into the lake with a hefty splash.

'Bloody marvellous!' hissed Paige.

'Beautiful,' muttered Wickham. 'Absolutely beautiful.'

'Again, please,' said Parker delightedly.

Almost instantly a second whirr began, and this was quickly followed by another energy sweep, resulting in the second stricken fighting machine's weapon being severed with the same precision. There followed the welcome second splash as another Martian heavy weapon hit the water. This resulted in a macabre stillness about the immediate vicinity. The far-off sounds of cannon and heat ray were still apparent – enhancing the night sky's fiery glow. But the flooded marshland of Observation Post Nine and the surrounding lake clung to its new eerie hush, that of a watery underworld where hidden alien ghouls were awaiting judgement.

'I bet the Martians are tucked up inside those capsules, getting ready for what's coming next,' hissed Parker.

'I hope the gits are stewing away nicely,' added Wickham.

'Well, let's not disappoint our unwelcome guests,' said Lieutenant Paige.

The young officer then raised himself to full height and reached up. He began to unscrew the conning tower hatch. Once done, he ascended the small ladder for a couple of rungs and pushed opened the lid. Boldly, he climbed out into the glowing night. The strange sickly-sweet smell of the red weed carried on the light breeze. His nostrils flared slightly and then he quickly dismissed the alien aroma. The odd-looking grasshopper men followed. For a moment, Paige surveyed the surrounding night's horizon. Flatlands still bathed in the glow of far-off battles and fiery destruction.

'I've just got to raise the walkway,' he said to the silent grasshopper men as they emerged onto the circular gantry just below the water level that was lapping around the tower. The shallow sloosh slapped against the rubber ankle area of their chest waders.

One of the grasshopper men pointed to Lieutenant Paige and tapped his gas mask. He said nothing but the indication was clear.

'Oh blast!' Paige scolded himself. 'Yes, what a bloody elementary mistake.'

The lieutenant pulled up his gas mask and fastened it firmly over his face. Then he proceeded with the task of hoisting the ropes that would raise the hidden scaffold walkway outside of the conning tower – the platform that led out into the shallow flooded fen.

Wickham popped his head out of the conning tower with his gas mask on. He mumbled through the breathing apparatus. 'Can I help, Sir?'

'Thank you, Corporal Wickham, I think I can manage this mesh platform,' answered Paige. 'It's placed below the flood water. We can lift this end up and out of the water. It hooks onto the rungs here, on the outer part of this tower.'

'A good idea,' mumbled Wickham through the mask. 'A slanting gantry that avoids the flood ditch where the piping is laid.'

'Lots of things have been taken into consideration,' replied Paige. 'Not bad for a rush job.'

Wickham nodded and looked to the inhuman faces of the silent bowler-hatted grasshopper men. The corporal realised he must have the same look while wearing his gas mask and pith helmet. 'Should any of us accompany the grasshopper men, Sir?'

'No, Wickham. The grasshopper men perform this function alone unless instructions change. This is a rehearsed drill. It's also the first time we have put it into proper practice. These chaps know what they're doing.'

Wickham stuttered nervously, 'Right-ho, Sir. They don't say much, do they?'

Paige ignored the corporal's remark. 'There! The gantry is hooked in place.'

The two grasshopper men cautiously climbed up onto the raised end of the sloping platform. For a moment they were out of the water. Then carefully each grasshopper man moved down the slope to re-enter the slosh and move deeper into the flooded lake water.

Wickham said, 'They are strangely dressed men, Sir. Their silence adds to the eerie look. I find them as creepy as the Martians.'

'Yes,' agreed Paige as he watched the peculiar grasshopper men descend the sloping platform. 'They look completely surreal in their normal black bowler hats and civilian ties, and this familiarity is set against macabre chest waders and bulky gas masks. That with the strange night sky makes for a mad painting. The sort one of those weird modern abstract artists might paint.'

'It all reminds me of a mediaeval painting I once saw a long time ago. It was a religious thing that was very disturbing. A vision of Hell and people walking within it.'

'And I suppose you see our grasshopper men in that painted landscape?' Paige nodded in understanding.

'Yes, Sir – sort of. Except that was fantasy. This is our reality, here.'

'Hell on Earth, Wickham. But we must still fight. One way or another, we must prevail.'

'Do you honestly think we can, Sir?'

'Yes, Wickham – I do. Something must come about. This is not our Hell. It must be for the Martians. Let them have Hell and all its evil legions descend upon them. Let all that is blighted and vile be upon them in this war of the worlds.'

'So, we are in the hands of these grasshopper men for the next part,' Wickham rasped through his air filter.

Each grasshopper man held his metal marker stake, the flag fluttering in each man's firm grip. Their other hand clutched their unholstered revolvers, barrels pointing upwards.

'Those puny guns offer a feeling of support and readiness, I suppose,' muttered Paige.

'A "feeling of support" is probably as good as it gets,' agreed Wickham. 'What good are those pistols?'

'They could be useful if the Martians emerge from their machines. Their horrible, mottled flesh can't stop bullets the way their machines do.'

Wickham replied, 'Well let's hope it becomes that minor consolation on the reassurance front. It would be splendid if a grasshopper man got to plug one of the Martian sods.'

They continued to watch as each grasshopper man stepped off the gantry. The sudden drop brought the water level up to the brave men's waists.

Lieutenant Paige nodded in satisfaction. 'It's as you said earlier, Corporal. This sloping platform definitely enables us to clear the deeper underwater ditch where the piping system runs beneath the dropped ground level. The platform serves a good purpose. Let's hope our grasshopper men do too.'

'I'm sure they will, Sir,' added Wickham.

'Yes, I hope so too, Wickham. These flood ditches that obscure our presence below water and earth level have afforded us this opportunity. The ditch line probably helped shield the shock of the island explosion as well.'

Paige and Wickham watched on as each grasshopper man looked up at the overwhelming domed effect of the glowing night sky.

'Little insects,' muttered Wickham.

'Against an overwhelming and uncaring panorama,' added Paige. 'A vista that pays no heed to such little mites like us.'

'Perhaps our unseen little mites can do more damage than expected?' Wickham said.

'Hope so, Corporal. We need some good results to come our way.'

The two grasshopper men conversed with one another briefly and then separated. In different directions, each man waded out further into the lake area of the flooded fen. One going to the first downed fighting machine while the other grasshopper man went to the second destroyed fighting machine.

Paige was full of admiration. 'Each brave man wades towards his goal or death. I'm certain there are Martians still alive within the machines.'

'That fellow has stopped, Sir!' Wickham pointed to the grasshopper man who had halted by the wreckage of the second fighting machine. The strange, masked man in his bowler hat held his flagged stake up for the lieutenant to see. Then the fellow slammed it down through the murky water and into the flooded earth below.

'That one is clearly marked,' Paige muttered to himself. He slowly waved his raised arm to acknowledge he could see the marker. Behind the grasshopper man was the partly submerged Martian container.

'For one dreadful moment I expected a trap-door might open,' Paige said.

'Expecting a Martian to emerge, Sir?'

'Yes. I know the aliens carry small heat ray weapons attached to cylinders – some type of energy container that is worn on the creatures' backs. I hope our chap returns quickly. We now have the location of the heat ray device, another Martian weapon we can press into our fighting service.'

'A few more wouldn't go amiss, Sir.'

Paige beckoned for the grasshopper man to return and was relieved when the man began to wade back in compliance.

'Well, that chap needed no further persuasion.' Paige sounded relieved.

As the lieutenant turned to the second grasshopper man, moving towards the first wrecked fighting machine, Wickham noticed black smoke spraying upwards from the second fighting machine's vent unit, gradually spreading. Threatening to smother the returning man.

'Blooming heck, Sir! Black smoke!' he hissed in alarm.

At that same moment the grasshopper man at the first stricken machine raised his flagged metal stake and slammed it down.

'Our other grasshopper man has located the next heat ray device, but there is black smoke emerging from his downed fighting machine too,' added Paige.

As the grasshopper man turned to get the lieutenant's acknowledgement, he saw the officer remonstrating excitedly. It caused the bowler-hatted man to look behind him, realising that something was causing such excitement. The thick black smoke quickly sank and spread about him, engulfing the man as he tried to make his way back.

A cacophony of noise from the conning tower's open lid caused the lieutenant to look up. More soldiers were coming out one by one with their rifles and bayonets fixed. He had to make way for them by stepping onto the narrow gantry and leaning to the wet rope rail for the line of soldiers to pass – anonymity via hidden faces in gas masks and pith helmets with back ribbon tassels fluttering in the night breeze. They made for an impressive-looking sight. Each Wake Man entered the sloshing water and waded out a little way before stopping.

'Come on now, lads, spread out in a line. Keep your distances,' called the corporal, who had lifted his mask up slightly to call the instructions. Paige stood aside and watched the rest of the Wake Men walk down the gantry slope and into the water. Ten of them in all.

Paige pulled his gas mask up and called, 'There's black smoke emitting from the first stricken vessel. One of the grasshopper men is within the cloud.' He then replaced his mask.

'Very good, Sir. We'll send a team forward,' the corporal shouted back. He quickly replaced his mask. The black smoke was spreading out.

The grasshopper man returning from the first marker got back to the line as his designated fighting machine also began to spew a trail of black poisonous smoke.

'Well, that's both of them emitting smoke. The Martians seem to know we're here,' said Paige nervously.

The distinct sound of an army-issue revolver rang out, overpowering the distant and far-off din of other battles. It was the gun of the grasshopper man who had been engulfed in the black smoke. He suddenly emerged in some haste. He was moving a little faster than the spreading cloud, mumbling something through his mask and gesticulating with his arms, trying to warn all of something afoot.

A thin beam of light shot out from the black smoke and struck the fleeing grasshopper man in the lower back. He seemed to twist as his midriff began to fizzle with an engulfing ring of sparks. There was an agonised ear-splitting scream as the devouring energy stripped the man's stomach away.

He twisted and almost split in two as his sizzling body splashed down into the water with a hiss.

'Groups of five – one section to Lance Corporal Hattie. The other with me,' shouted the corporal.

With well-practised discipline, the Wake Men formed two groups of five, each facing one of the stricken fighting machines engulfed in a protective cloud of black poisonous smoke. All Wake Men held their rifles at thirty degrees with bayonets fixed and ready.

'Spread out! Keep your distances!' called the corporal, daring to once again lift the front of his mask slightly.

The two lines of men complied as another beam of thin gleaming energy shot out from the black smoke. It hit nothing and shot harmlessly over the expanse of water.

'Oh my God!' Lieutenant Paige muttered. He watched in wide-eyed astonishment. The vocal corporal fell in with four men and he noticed a lance corporal among the second set of four. Every Wake Man was wearing his gas mask and appeared ready to enter the black poisonous smoke. He had heard of the drill but never witnessed it.

'Before my very eyes, the entire thing looks suicidal,' he said.

'Especially after seeing the demise of the grasshopper man by Martian small-arms fire, Sir,' Wickham agreed.

'If the wretched man has been slain by a mere Martian feeler-held device, what chance do these men have?'

'Maybe they can evade the small-arms heat ray better than the huge things the tripods carry, Sir?'

'I hope you are correct, Wickham. It's not as powerful a weapon as the fighting machine's actual device, but it certainly seems capable of killing in the same way when hitting human flesh.'

Then, to Lieutenant Paige's and Corporal Wickham's utter disbelief, they heard the Wake Men corporal's loud and confident call. An angry instruction roaring through the night.

'WAKE MEN! WAKE MEN – ADVANCE!'

Five men moved forward, five bayonets at thirty degrees, wading towards the expanding black cloud where the grasshopper man had recently been killed.

A second booming order came from Lance Corporal Hattie of the other five-man column. A confident no-nonsense instruction.

'WAKE MEN! WAKE MEN – ADVANCE!'

The surviving grasshopper man stood aside as the second group of Wake Men, bayonets aloft, waded towards the second expanding cloud of black smoke coming from the other stricken tripod machine. Each group disappeared inside their designated spreading dark cloud.

The sound of sporadic rifle fire instantly followed. The fizz of small heat ray weapons spat from the black obscurity and an agonised human scream ripped through the illuminated night air. More orders were called out. Further rifle fire followed inside each wall of black vapour. The unseen cacophony of bullets and alien energy hissing within the murky confines.

A strange animal yell was heard. An alien roar of pain from an unseen Martian creature.

'That one has been struck by a wicked human-made projectile, Wickham,' said Lieutenant Paige gleefully.

'My heart bleeds for the poor fellow,' replied Wickham, capturing the sudden upbeat mood. The sporadic fire was not letting up and the fizz of hand-held heat ray was diminishing within both black clouds.

'What the blazes is happening, Lieutenant Paige?' asked Dr Cheema as he emerged from the conning tower. He was followed by Miss Clairmont, each carrying their canvas medical satchels and wearing gas masks.

'It's a blooming great shoot-out between Wake Men and the Martians,' replied Paige in delightful admiration. 'Our chaps are attacking the Martians in their machines. The things are returning heat ray fire.'

'Are we winning?' asked the doctor, equally as mesmerised at the sounds of rifle and energy fire. He looked up and about at the panoramic scene of Hell on Earth. This was their little enclave of the wicked new realm.

'I honestly don't know, Dr Cheema.'

From out of the black smoke came muffled human shouts and instructions. Another barrage of rifle fire and a second unhuman scream.

'I sincerely hope that's one of the Martian blighters,' said Dr Cheema.

'I think it is,' replied Miss Clairmont enthusiastically through the rasping ventilator. 'Come on, our boys. Let them have it – good and proper.' She punched the air and then had to contain her excitement when she noticed Dr Cheema, Lieutenant Paige and Corporal Wickham staring back at her through their gas masks.

'I say, dashed good show, Miss Clairmont,' said Paige admiringly. 'I think our chaps are giving the blighters a thing or two to think about.'

The surviving grasshopper man came up the ramp and called over to Lieutenant Paige. 'Sir. We can retrieve a heat ray device from just inside the smoke. It will need at least two men to carry it and one guide.'

'Well then, you can be the guide. Corporal Wickham and one other shall accompany you. I'll go for the other with a couple of fellows. Where's Parker?' Paige muttered and saw the soldier staring out through the observation slit. 'Out you come, Parker. Not much use there, lad.'

CHAPTER 8

AMID IT ALL

Parker emerged with the two railway workers, Mike and Bill. All were wearing the regulation gas masks. Each man clambered down the outside of the conning tower to stand on the tower's circular gantry that ran just below the water level – their waders being put to good use.

'Right then, Parker, I want you and Mike to accompany me into the fringe of the black smoke over there. There is a marker placed by a useable heat ray device.'

'Should I not go with you, Sir?' asked the grasshopper man.

'No, I want you to go with Corporal Wickham here, and the rail worker called Bill. I do hope you will agree to this, Bill?'

'Yes, Sir. Of course, I will,' replied the station hand.

'Splendid! Now Corporal Wickham knows roughly where the marker is. Not far inside the fringe of the dissipating black smoke. You can remember can't you, Wickham?'

'I can, Sir,' he replied. There was an infectious enthusiasm as the surrounding sporadic fire of conflict continued. Another alien scream emerged from the black cloud. 'That's three! By my reckoning there's only one left if all four survived the machines' collapse.'

'We must work on the principle that all four have,' added Paige with his eyebrow raised. He turned to Dr Cheema and Miss Clairmont and continued, 'There is a protocol to try and retrieve Martian dead. You may see Wake Men emerge from the black cloud carrying one, or with knowledge of where one is. We need to get any specimen over this pipe to the island where our artillery unit is. I think tarpaulin has already been erected with red weed camouflage. This is where you and Miss Clairmont can go about dissecting the Martians. They will be dead, obviously, but if we can learn anything of value…?'

'I'm sure we can learn a wealth of things, Lieutenant Paige,' Dr Cheema replied. He was now visibly excited by the way the battle seemed to be going.

Paige turned to Miss Clairmont and added, 'And I trust your past expertise in the field of dissecting assistance will be fine with alien life form—'

'It will, indeed, Lieutenant Paige,' Miss Clairmont cut in and smiled politely.

Everyone was feeling as though they had a sense of purpose in the middle of a huge achievement. Two downed fighting machines and a group of soldiers entering the wreckage to fight close quarters with an enemy that recently seemed untouchable.

'Well then, let's cut to the chase,' continued Lieutenant Paige. 'Parker and Mike with me. Corporal Wickham and our grasshopper man with Bill. You chaps know what to do as well.'

Cautiously, each group boarded the inclined platform. They walked down and slowly waded out into the lake. Before them was the wall of poisonous fumes hovering above the shining lake water. Muffled calls and sporadic shots continued within the dark mist as each retrieve group made for their respective locations. Lieutenant Paige's crew made for a marker that Dr Cheema could just about see on the fringe of the murky haze.

He looked to Miss Clairmont and said, 'I think that's their marker flag by the periphery of the poisonous mist. Just over there.'

'Oh yes, I think you are correct, Dr Cheema.' She looked to the second group, headed by Corporal Wickham. 'I can't see the flag that Corporal Wickham is searching for. The one from the first downed Martian vessel. I suppose he has a rough idea. Maybe he saw it placed before the vapour came out of the wrecked tripod.'

A few quick-fire rifle shots rang out from the cloud, and suddenly two Wake Men emerged walking backwards. They were dragging a grey bodily mass – a lumpy form with tendrils floating in the lake water. Then Lance Corporal Hattie followed, and Miss Clairmont heard the man call out.

'Where's the other one?' he called through his gas mask.

'It got away,' came the muffled reply from one of the Wake Men, dragging the alien corpse. 'It's not in the cloud, it went into the water. I think it's out here somewhere.'

Lieutenant Paige and his retrieval group watched as more Wake Men emerged from the lethal haze of their destroyed fighting machine. Two groups of two Wake Men, each dragging the bulging grey configuration of an unrecognisable grey body mass. More limp appendages floated in the lake water as the soldiers gingerly walked backwards.

'Look!' called Miss Clairmont, pointing towards the other black cloud where Corporal Wickham, Bill and the grasshopper man emerged carrying their heat ray device.

'Excellent!' exclaimed Dr Cheema. 'That's both parties returning.'

Miss Clairmont beamed with delight too. Lieutenant Paige was also returning with a heat ray device. 'All in all, one might say it was a sound night of plunder for this little outpost, Dr Cheema.'

'Indeed, you are correct, Miss Clairmont. Do you mind if I go down to the end of the platform to help those men with those dead Martians? We're going to have to bring them up and over the piping. Our tent is on the island opposite.'

'I know, Doctor. Please do go, by all means.'

The doctor climbed up onto the ramp and gingerly made his way down into the lake water. He was pleased to see that the loud corporal and his three surviving Wake Men were the first to near the ramp. They had made splendid progress. Two men apiece, dragging their dead Martian burdens.

'Here, let me help you,' he said, looking down at the dead abomination. The creature's hide was cracked and wrinkled like that of an elephant. Yet the form was like a giant misshaped butterbean that was going a bad grey colour. Tendrils with three tiny-fingered appendages floated limply from the Martian's bulk. There were warts and carbuncles in the mottled epidermis and big bulging glazed eyes with huge yellow irises and dark pupils. Beyond the sickly yellow irises was the ill-looking off-white sclera riddled with masses of thin red veins. Below and between the dead eyes was the ridged pattern that led to a sharp-looking raptor-like beak.

Dr Cheema gasped. 'I've never seen one of these things before, but it looks unwell.'

'Well, it is dead, Doctor,' replied the Wake Men corporal a tad sarcastically.

'If we could dispense with the flippancy, Corporal,' Dr Cheema scolded. 'This thing's eyes were probably this colour before it was killed. I'm actually saying the thing was definitely unhealthy before it stopped one of your Wake Men's bullets and thus making its already dreadful circumstance considerably worse.'

'I think it stopped two, at least, Doctor,' added another Wake Man. 'I've counted two bullet holes and loads of bayonet wounds. The thing's back is a pulped mess where the bullets have hit the front and exited from the rear. Look at its chest area. Like shooting a giant prize-winning marrow. Neat hole one side and a blooming rotten mess at the rear where the bullets ripped out of the blubber.'

'Blubber?' Dr Cheema frowned. 'Yes, I suppose it is for want of a better word. The wretched creature wouldn't have known what hit it as the projectiles entered then exited via the back.'

Two Wake Men from the other group approached with Lance Corporal Hattie. He said, his voice muffled by the gas mask, 'This is so, Dr Cheema. Our one was trying to get back to its downed fighting machine, but the lads fell upon it with bayonets just as it reached the hull.'

'There is another Martian unaccounted for,' added another of his Wake Men. 'It might be dead in the stricken machine.'

'Might, is not definite,' said Dr Cheema. 'We may need to explore the machine once the black mist has cleared.'

Lance Corporal Hattie added a further problem to consider: 'It may also have got away. Perhaps out here somewhere?'

Up by the conning tower, Miss Clairmont looked along the gently sloping walkway at the minor commotion between Dr Cheema and the return-ing Wake Men with their captured dead Martians. Corporal Wickham, the grasshopper man and Bill had come to the group carrying their captured bulky heat ray weapon. There was a small gathering of Wake Men forming around the linking walkway – so many things of interest as all the men began to soak up the prizes before them. She was about to climb up out of the ankle-deep water around the circular platform. Once on the top of the ramp sup-port she could walk down to join the commotion.

Dr Cheema stopped her when he called back, 'We're coming back, Miss Clairmont. Please don't enter the water yet.'

Miss Clairmont felt slightly put out by the instruction. But, before she could act, her attention was diverted by a splash along the underwater pipeline behind her. She managed to turn, but the whole episode happened so quick there was barely time to register the danger she was in.

Like a banshee from Hell, the abomination erupted out of the water. A set of hideous yellow eyes. A huge open raptor-like beak, emitting an enraged high-pitched squeal. The hideous heaving hide of mottled alien flesh thumped against her. She fell beneath the enraged assault, the wind knocked out of her. Gruesome appendages wrapped about her body while she choked and spluttered for breath beneath the murky lake water. The gas mask was ripped away during the struggle as her chest waders filled with water and began dragging her down between the curve of the underwater pipe and the submerged embankment. The revolting grey epidermis was trying to smother her petrified face. Twisting and turning amid the bubbles, she managed to battle the restraining tentacles and clamber over the alien mass. Pushing herself away, she managed to get her head to the surface. She was choking and spluttering but somehow managed to grab part of the upper sloping gantry while feeling her waterlogged waders dragging her down. Then her scream tore out amid the human calls of panic.

Her shriek ended abruptly. Her reason kicked in. The need to take a deep breath! She filled her lungs with the sickly-sweet air, polluted by red weed, just in time as another appendage wrapped about her mouth and began to heave her down. She tightened her grip and held on for dear life. Feet rapidly approached along the shuddering framework and her last fleeting vision was of Dr Cheema's green turban and gas mask, one hand clasping his medical satchel while the other fired a revolver. Behind and to one side, she made out the pith helmet of Corporal Wickham complete with gas mask and raised rifle. On the other side of the doctor, she made out the form of the grasshopper man in his bowler hat and gas mask, also firing a revolver.

Panic set in as she managed to gulp another breath of air before her strength deserted her. Again, she was beneath the water, staring into a gigantic yellow eye with a large black pupil. Her heart was thumping as she tried to control the panic within. They were coming to her aid. She must hold on. She could hear the distorted sound of shots from above and sensed rather than saw soldiers about her as the grotesque eye and mottled grey corpse receded from her.

Coughing and spluttering, she was hauled up out of the water to lie immobile on the lookout tower gantry. Dr Cheema was grasping her firmly and trying to reassure her.

'You are safe, Miss Clairmont. The thing is taken care of,' he said and then hugged her. 'You are safe,' he repeated.

'I need to get these waders off,' she replied in panic. 'They're full of water.'

'Turn her upside down!' shouted a Wake Man.

Miss Clairmont suffered further indignation as she was hauled up and firmly held upside down in the most inappropriate way. Water cascaded out of her chest waders into the shallow sloosh around the surrounding gantry, the dirty cascading liquid making her splutter more. Finally, the torrid rush began to subside. Miss Clairmont was hanging head down and laughing – a nervous yet relieved laughter at the stupidity and necessity of her predicament. It was over now.

Gently, Miss Clairmont found herself turned upright to a sitting position.

'Are you alright, Miss Clairmont?' Dr Cheema was full of concern.

'I think there have been occasions when I've felt better, Dr Cheema. But right now, I'll settle for being damp, cold and traumatised – yet still living and breathing.'

'Splendid, Miss Clairmont. That's the spirit.' Dr Cheema was most relieved.

As she shivered and gasped for breath, the new development of the horror played out. The struggle between the Wake Men, led by Corporal Wickham, and her Martian attacker moved across the water, from the submerged pipe to the bottom of the slanting gantry. Abhorrent squealing and desperate flailing appendages splashed about frantically.

The repulsive alien's body mass was mostly hidden by the backs of three battling soldiers. Some of the struggling creature's dexterous tentacles became entwined about the ropes of the gantry frame. Other appendages feebly tried to parry the assaulting Wake Men's bayonets. Three slimy wispy extremities, on one such feeler, desperately clasped one of the rifle bayonets. The pathetic digits were instantly sliced off with one quick twist of the blade, blood oozing from the three severed stumps. Each soldier raised his rifle high, bringing the blade down with brutal force. Stabbing, thrusting and twisting the wicked implements in the terrified Martian's tortured being. The chaotic violence of humanity put the hideous abhorrence to task. Repeatedly skewering, Corporal Wickham and two Wake Men wore gleeful hate-filled smiles. Red blood splashed, like that of any human, from violent rupturing stab wounds. Roars of gratification bellowed as the unyielding attack continued. Even when the Martian stopped screaming the assault went on.

'There will be nothing left of it to dissect,' spluttered Miss Clairmont as she was supported, while trying to stand, by Dr Cheema.

'I think we may have to let the soldiers get this one out of their system, Miss Clairmont. We still have three more to dissect.'

'What hideous things,' she hissed, her repulsion growing.

More Wake Men from Lance Corporal Hattie's team came up the gantry carrying their dead Martian's heat device and back cylinder unit.

One of them called, 'This is one of their small heat rays and cylinder machines. We found it inside the smoke.'

Lieutenant Paige quickened his wading through the water to the gantry. He passed the angry group, still bayoneting the already dead Martian, his concern being for Miss Clairmont. Upon reaching the upper section by the lookout cone, he climbed over onto the slightly submerged platform surrounding the lookout section.

'My word, Miss Clairmont. You look shaken up. Are you physically hurt?' he asked with genuine concern.

'I'm alright now, Lieutenant Paige.' She stood upright and shivered in the night's breeze, but she knew her strong resolve was returning. 'Dr Cheema and I have work to do.'

'Corporal!' Lieutenant Paige tutted, appearing rude as he turned away from Miss Clairmont. He held out his hands for emphasis at the three Wake Men by the dead Martian. They had abruptly stopped midway in the throes of further violence. Each was momentarily poised with bayonet-fixed rifles held high.

'Yes, Sir?' replied Wickham, sheepishly wiping the wicked grin from his face and holding his bloodied rifle and bayonet above his head.

'Please could you stop bayoneting our Martian? The thing is well and truly dead, and we would like to leave some of the blighter for Dr Cheema and Miss Clairmont to dissect.'

'Yes, Sir! Very good, Sir – sorry, Sir.' Wickham snapped out of his angry revenge, as did the two Wake Men alongside him. 'Got a bit carried away, Sir.'

'Of course, you did, Corporal. Right then,' continued Paige. 'Could you raise the gantry ropes on the other side of the conning tower? That one needs to be hooked up and then we can get the dead Martians and other bits over to the island mass – make them ready for Dr Cheema, Miss Clairmont and our two station workers-cum-medical assistants, Mike and Bill. The good doctor and his assistant are keen to do a little slicing of their own and would consider it awfully nice if you could leave them a little something to study.'

'Will do, Sir,' Wickham called back.

Paige turned and smiled to Miss Clairmont. 'Please accept my humble apologies for being so abrupt with the chaps, Miss Clairmont. It was not my intention to be rude or dismissive to you.'

Miss Clairmont giggled. Her hair was wet and bedraggled as she stood before the officer. 'That's perfectly fine, Lieutenant Paige. After all, I'm sure Dr Cheema and I would appreciate some of the Martian to dissect.'

Dr Cheema decided to speak up in defence of Miss Clairmont's ordeal. 'I think we might need to let—'

'No, Dr Cheema,' Miss Clairmont interrupted. 'I am anxious to assist you in this matter as soon as possible. The last thing I want to do is dwell on this event while resting. I do not think it will do me any good, but I thank you kindly for your concern.'

Lieutenant Paige seemed to understand what Miss Clairmont meant, but he felt compelled to ask again out of politeness. 'If you are sure, Miss Clairmont, but no one would think ill of you after such an ordeal. You can rest if you wish?'

'No thank you, Lieutenant Paige.' She looked to Dr Cheema and said, 'Is there lighting inside the tent?'

'There is, Miss Clairmont, and very good cover too. None of the inner lighting can get out. We have several layers of tarpaulin to work under, and it's all covered in red weed.'

'Let's get to it then, Dr Cheema,' she replied.

Lieutenant Paige was already raising the gantry on the other side of the conning tower while Wake Men manoeuvred their Martian corpses onto the new raised scaffold to carry the alien burdens across to the island, where the artillery unit and tarpaulin tent was set up.

CHAPTER 9

MAKING USE OF EVERY CAPTURED SPOIL

'I don't know what is more interesting,' said Parker to Wickham, looking out at the Wake Men working around one of the wrecked fighting machines. 'The morning seems serene. It's hard to believe it was so hectic during the night. Just look at it all now. The day is glorious. We can see for miles all over the fen and there's not a Martian fighting machine to be seen.'

'Still the rumble of guns to the north, but they seem far off,' agreed Wickham. 'The Fens seem like a little out-of-the-way safe zone now. We have those two lifeless fighting machines rusting away in the lake out there, now. Not threatening and they are in sight.'

'Yes, and that means they don't count anymore, as far as danger goes! May they continue to rot away, forever and a day,' said Parker, laughing.

'I would like to have been a fly on the wall when Lieutenant Paige was discussing the downed fighting machines and the capture of heat ray weapons with Colonel Hereward Blake. I wonder what the old man had to say?'

Parker sighed contentedly. 'The colonel is out there with the Wake Men now. He seems rather pleased about things.'

'Yes, but is it the construction work they're doing or the result of yesterday night's battle?'

Parker shrugged. 'Well, I would think it's a bit of both. I reckon the colonel will be rather pleased with his Wake Men, all ways considered. We did do very well, and the lads out there now are going about their work in a very excited way.'

'A fine little catch of achievements, I would say,' said Wickham.

'And we mustn't forget the study of Martians,' added Parker. 'Dr Cheema and Miss Clairmont have been out there all night and now it's late morning. I'm sure they are finding out a few things too.'

'I'm wondering what our Colonel Hereward Blake is going to do about the two machines he has at his disposal?' Wickham nodded towards the observation slit. Outside, by the wrecked island that had been planted with explosives and fireworks, the Wake Men engineers were raising a scaffold of telegraph poles, criss-crossed to form a strong support.

'It's Colonel Henry Edward Blake,' retorted Parker.

'Get with the banter, you bally great Gladys. It's the colonel's nickname,' whispered Wickham. 'You know that, so don't keep correcting me. If you don't like it just stay silent and get on with your knitting. Stop acting like a big girl's blouse.'

'Blooming heck! There was a few below the belt insults in that little sentence,' replied Parker, pretending to be hurt by the words.

'You'll get over it.' Wickham smiled as he returned his scrutiny to the scaffold tower that was being constructed. 'I once saw a picture in a history book. There was a siege tower on wheels being rolled forward to breach a castle wall. The building work reminds me of one of those siege towers. Those rafts that the soldiers are punting across the lake – they're full of more telegraph poles, enough to build another one of those towers. I think they are going to raise one of the fighting machines, then use those constructions either side for support.'

'Support towers, aye? Where did the Wake Men get those rafts from?' Parker asked, also intently peering through the observation slit.

'I think they're getting them from the railway yard in March. They're using the rafts to carry the cargo. The railway is probably of little use now. It's all rather clever really.' Wickham was very impressed.

'But the Martians destroyed March yesterday, or so I thought.' Parker sighed.

'It's still smouldering over there.' Wickham scratched his chin and removed his pith helmet briefly to run his fingers through his ruffled greasy hair. 'I suppose a unit or two went back once these now wrecked fighting machines moved on. The raft platforms were probably scattered about the burning rail yard. Even if the place is burning, I'm sure the survey teams found it easy to retrieve the rafts. They have barrels on each corner to give them buoyancy. Probably knocked that design up there and then. It all looks like shoddy work. Still, the rafts are doing their job and that's what counts, I suppose.'

Parker sighed. 'I was wondering why they were bringing all those blooming telegraph poles across to the firework island. I kept asking myself, "What use will they be?"'

Wickham sniggered. 'Well, I'm not absolutely sure, but I think my guess is correct on the scaffold tower idea. After all, they seem at great pains to bring them here. They must have a good reason.'

'I hope we get to see them raise one of the tripods,' said Parker with new-found enthusiasm.

'That would be a tale,' agreed Wickham.

The lid of the conning tower opened and the clear blue sky allowed a moment of pleasure for the two lookout men. Mike, the station worker, looked in.

'How are you lads this morning? The guns seem to be firing much further north, but there are still fighting machines to the east. Around King's Lynn.'

'Seems a bit quiet around here, especially after last night,' added Wickham. 'Is there much going on with Dr Cheema and Miss Clairmont?'

'I should say,' replied Mike as he climbed down the short ladder and onto the inner lookout gantry, his wet waders dripping all about the place. He lingered to have a brief word with the soldiers. 'I've been sent back to collect a few things from their hospital. Some solutions in a cabinet. They wrote them down for me. They have microscopes that can look at germs and things. Tiny germs get magnified under these microscope tools. All very clever stuff, you know. They want other solutions to put on these little glass slides containing germs. They want to find out what type of germs the Martians are carrying.'

'And is that it?' asked Parker, a little disappointed.

'Of course not. Dr Cheema and Miss Clairmont have been getting rather excited about various diseases found in each Martian's blood. Our invaders seem to be picking up everything I can think of

and things I've never heard of. Honestly, one of the
dead Martians has syphilis.'

'How can it catch that?' Parker ridiculed Mike
in disbelief.

'Well, Bill asked that very question when he
heard Miss Clairmont say such a thing. The lady
said that Martians suck blood. If they suck the
blood of someone with syphilis, the blighters would
be able to catch it. Honestly, the doctor and his
assistant are flabbergasted by the various diseases
that the Martians have. I've heard them mention so
many things. Salmonella, hepatitis, tuberculosis,
and Miss Clairmont said something called Lyme
disease, from tick bites in the Martian's skin. Also,
the words "carbon based". I'm not sure if that's a
disease or something the Martians are made of.
I don't know what it all means, but Dr Cheema
explained something to Bill and me. He said that
if the Martians, on their operating tables, were not
killed by our Wake Men last night, they wouldn't
have lived long afterwards because of these ill-
nesses. The Martians seem to be catching every
type of germ or virus our Mother Earth can offer.
Even that thing you bayoneted up beyond recognition was full of different blood infections. All the
germs of Earth are having a field day with these
creatures. Dr Cheema says these many contamina-
tions must be running wild among all the Martians

inside their machines. He seems to think it's the blood-sucking of humans and animals they catch that has caused this. The vile practice is slowly killing them. Not every food source is healthy, and our Martian invaders don't seem to have grasped such dangers.'

'Did Dr Cheema mention how long these germs would take to kill our uninvited visitors?' asked Wickham. His interest was slowly simmering. There was logic in the rumour, and he doubted that Mike could make such a thing up. They were all laymen, but some of the infections were known to him. Many were not, but if the unknown afflictions were bad ones too, then all well and good. He added excitedly, 'Bloody germs. Who would have thought of that? Yet germs can be lethal if these Martians don't know how to treat them. For all their monstrous killing machines, they can't stop tiny germs.'

Mike made for the main gantry ladder. 'I'll tell you blokes more later. I'm going to get the bottles of solution for Dr Cheema. I think they may find more diseases inside the blood and skin of the dead Martians.' He disappeared as he climbed down into the hollow water tank and said good morning to Sergeant Curtis. Then Mike went into the pipe tunnel towards the hospital tank.

'Can you believe that?' said Parker dismissively.

Wickham was frowning. 'Actually, I can. I just don't want to build my hopes up too much. But such a thing could be big. Pestilence and disease might be the biggest wallop we could give the Martians. Something we have all overlooked. Soldiers don't think about such things.'

'I'm more excited by what that lot are doing with the blooming telegraph poles.' Parker returned his attention to the observation slit where a group of Wake Men engineers were hard at work. They were erecting a second scaffold structure, just as Wickham speculated earlier. Also, around one of the fallen fighting machines, more Wake Men were calmly securing ropes. They worked tirelessly under the clear blue summer sky. The distant *boom* of far-off artillery persisted, but it was many miles away and none of the soldiers seemed concerned.

Wickham grinned. 'I think that some devious plan is afoot. I'm certain our Colonel Hereward Blake is going to hoist a fighting machine back up with one of the captured heat ray devices fixed to it. Lieutenant Paige seems to think so too. He says the colonel's plan may work.'

'So, you never guessed,' Parker retorted. 'You knew because Lieutenant Paige informed you.'

'The lieutenant only gave me little snippets of news here and there. I worked the rest out,' replied Wickham flippantly.

Parker chuckled at the corporal's antics. 'Well, the colonel seems to have got a few things right so far. But I'm still nervous. It smells of another lark like the one we went through last night. It was rather scary at times.'

'It's nice to see your honesty is bubbling to the surface on the fighting front. A mixture of admiration but an experience we wouldn't like to go through again.'

'I think there's a compliment in there somewhere.' Parker laughed.

Wickham smiled as he watched the Wake Men going about their construction. 'Lieutenant Paige is of the opinion that our colonel wants that big four-crew fighting machine. The one that went to Wisbech and moved on to destroy other things somewhere else. The colonel is stubborn in his belief that this bigger Martian vessel will return to search for the two we have felled. The absence of such machines will not pass unnoticed.'

'Oh, me – Gawd!' replied Parker.

'Oh, *my God*!' corrected Wickham.

'That's what I said.' Parker was a little indignant.

'Well, what do you mean by "Oh, my God"?' Wickham wanted to know more of the young soldier's thoughts.

'I think I know now! The mist is beginning to clear and I don't think I like what I can see. Our

Wake Men *are* making the frame and scaffolding gear to hoist up a fallen tripod. When the big Daddy four-Martian machine comes along, our commandeered thing is going to fire back at it. Please tell me the colonel is not going to try that one.' Suddenly Parker had lost his sense of humour.

Wickham sniggered. 'I've got the strangest of feelings that the colonel is going to try exactly that. I think it might work too.'

'Blimey! The old boy certainly likes to give it a go. Well, perhaps he gets us to give it a go. I hadn't laid eyes on this Colonel Hereward Blake, as you like to call him. Not until this morning, that is. Have you seen him before?'

Wickham shook his head as he watched the eccentric colonel directing things. 'No, I haven't, but Lieutenant Paige has on a number of occasions. He was summoned by the top brass after our final battle with the Martian crew last night.'

'The Martians that Dr Cheema and Miss Clairmont are slicing up on their little operating table, as we speak?'

'The very ones,' answered Wickham. 'When Lieutenant Paige returned, he mentioned that Wake Men engineers will be constructing something to lift up one of these fighting machines. He also added that one of the captured heat ray guns would be re-attached to the elevated machine.'

'How comes you get all this information, and I don't get to hear it from the horse's mouth?' Parker sounded put out.

'Well, Lieutenant Paige told Sergeant Curtis. Sergeant Curtis then told yours truly, as in me. He's my horse's mouth while Colonel Blake is the lieutenant's horse's mouth, so to speak…'

'Alright! Next, you're going to tell me you're *my* horse's mouth.'

Wickham gave Parker a condescending smile. 'And for you, at this time, Corporal Wickham – as in yours truly – is as good as it gets.'

'Well, Corporal Wickham, you're a real packet of giggles with it all. We are going to fight monster Martian machines with another wish and a kiss to the sky. I can't wait.'

'Stop whingeing, Parker – you'll bloody love it when people ask to hear your story in the future. You'll be really bigging your part up.' Wickham couldn't help chuckling. Parker often had a dour expression, even when he was being humorous.

'I feel like I'm the eternal victim of circumstance.'

'Well, try and get on board with it all. Grab a slice of enthusiasm. We downed two of the blighters last night and we may get a few more yet. We'll get ready for the next visit.' He tapped Parker on the shoulder and climbed up through the circular port lid to breathe in the summer air.

Parker sarcastically called up, 'It leaves me with that right old feeling of expected party excitement.'

'It may be just that,' Wickham called down, surveying the surrounding Fenlands. The lake looked rather calm in the bright summer's day. Every little island above the flood water was sporting the parasitic Martian red weed but it did not spoil the view entirely. Small streams of smoke rose from various points on the horizon. He could turn in every direction and see a thin flume dissipating before the overwhelmingly blue sky. Something Earthlier and something winning over the alien invasion – just for the moment.

The water lapped against the lower part of the conning tower and he looked over at the Wake Men standing in the gleaming lake water beneath the serene blue of the sky. They had briefly stopped their work – for a moment, each Wake Man stood waist-deep in water, looking up at two hawks. Each raptor's wings serenely spread as the beautiful creatures glided around, watching one another on opposite sides of their spiralling climb. It was a moment, but it brought a little delight to all the soldiers.

'What's going on?' asked Parker as he managed to stand up beside Corporal Wickham.

'Just watching a couple of hawks doing their courting ritual flight,' replied Wickham.

'Oh!' Parker gasped in wonder. 'That is a sight for sore eyes. They look wonderful.'

'A touch of summer normality,' added Wickham.

'We can't let the Martians take all this from us.'

Wickham smiled. 'Maybe we won't. One way or another, we must find a way not to let them do such a thing.'

All continued to watch as the majestic hawks climbed higher and circled off and over the water-logged fenland, uncaring of the dilemma below.

Wickham breathed in the summer air. 'It's hard to believe, but we are inside Martian conquered territory. A pocket of resistance that's living on borrowed time – most probably.'

'That's the way, Corporal Wickham. Cheer me up good and proper,' Parker replied dryly.

CHAPTER 10

THE MEETING OF OPINIONS

Miss Clairmont put aside the discomfort of sweating. The wet and dirty clothes under her horrid, sticky chest waders were no different from every other member of the group. No one was spared the inconvenience. Soon, she may be able to go along the underwater pipe section to the ablution area and clean herself up. For now, she had to put up with the feeling of her own personal mistreatment.

She tried to focus on other things, something interesting and uplifting beyond her and Dr Cheema's assisted medical discoveries. She was delighted and astonished by the huge scaffold work the Wake Men engineers had constructed on the other island – the firework-rigged land beyond the observation tower and its underwater piping system.

The man-made flood lapped above her narrow waist as she waded through the water. It was the afternoon and the lamplight work, inside the tarpaulin tent, was finished. They were overjoyed to emerge into the unexpected and beautiful summer day, after hours of engrossing work. The artillery men, standing by their red weed-covered field gun, had bid them good day. It all seemed so polite and standardly British. The clear blue sky lent a wonderful feeling of normality. It temporarily removed her fear of Martian invaders. She had happily followed Dr Cheema over the marshy grass and into the lake water to make for the red weed-covered conning tower of Observation Post Nine.

Her vision continued to roam and she had to say so. 'Everywhere seems pleasant and warm in the expanse of our man-made lake. Here and there, little dotted islands. Just like the one we're leaving.'

Dr Cheema smiled. 'Very beautiful now. Little islands rising above the gleaming little breakers.'

'It aids us,' Miss Clairmont replied enthusiastically. 'Keeps us in fine spirits because of the medical discoveries. Such a beautiful summer sky to garnish our optimistic feelings.'

They held their satchels above their heads as they made their way towards the narrow gantry leading up to the cone-shaped open hatch of the tower, their collection of written files and results inside – a treasure of interest.

'I think Lieutenant Paige has spotted us making for the observation tower,' said Dr Cheema with an air of satisfaction.

'Is that him by the open lid?' Miss Clairmont squinted as she tried to peer amid the sparkles reflecting from the gentle sun-kissed waves.

'It is indeed, Miss Clairmont, and I think we may have to enlighten our young officer of our findings immediately.'

'I wouldn't be too surprised if Mike and Bill may have already spread a few rumours. Lieutenant Paige is wearing a smile of expectation. He seems to know we have exciting news.'

Dr Cheema chuckled. 'Well, I suppose we'll have to let our assistants do their rumour-spreading. We were rather vocal in our delight and discoveries.'

'You seem very pleased with yourselves,' Lieutenant Paige called from the top of the narrow red weed-infested conning tower, his moustache neatly kicking up into a smile.

'We are rather pleased with our finding, Lieutenant,' Dr Cheema called back delightedly.

'We think you might be too,' added Miss Clairmont, smiling.

'Splendid stuff,' replied Paige. 'Can we talk in the hospital tank. It's empty, but we do have two new medical staff coming to take up the position in a few hours' time.'

'Therefore, we are no longer required as medical staff?' asked Dr Cheema.

'Maybe if the demand arises in the future, but for the moment, I think your research in the autopsy area is of greater value now, Dr Cheema. Colonel Blake is very excited and wants to see you. I think he has a number of questions he would like to ask concerning these alien dissections.'

Dr Cheema and Miss Clairmont reached the slanting gantry and began to come up out of the lake, making towards the conning tower's open hatch as their wet waders dripped with lake water. Lieutenant Paige had climbed down inside to allow them easy access.

Swiftly, both Miss Clairmont and the doctor managed to climb into the service hatch, making sure their gas masks, swinging around their necks, were clasped with one hand while awkwardly descending the small inner ladder onto the gantry platform. Here, Wickham, Parker and Lieutenant Paige were wearing the most welcoming of expressions.

'Are we a sight for sore eyes then, Lieutenant?' Dr Cheema smiled. He was in a very positive mood.

'Well, to be honest the tank is alive with rumour and speculation concerning the Martian specimens that you and Miss Clairmont have examined.'

Lieutenant Paige was being a little careful and did not mention where such speculation came from.

'From Mike and Bill, no doubt?' added Miss Clairmont, looking amused and refreshingly light-hearted about the matter.

'Well, to be fair, my two chaps have been pumping them for snippets of information every time your lads came inside.' Paige nodded to Wickham and Parker. 'Everyone is excited by what they've heard.'

Dr Cheema smiled. 'And with good reason, Lieutenant. I am pleased to say that our Martian invaders are susceptible to almost everything we can think of. Let's proceed to the hospital tank. Is Colonel Blake there?'

'Not yet, Doctor.' Paige pointed out of the observer slit where the Wake Men were continuing to fasten ropes to one of the partially raised tripods. Above and either side of the slowly rising fighting machine was the brace of sturdy constructions – two giant wooden scaffold towers, shaped like colossal goal posts. Each top post had a strong pulley system. Each tower had taut supporting ropes attached from the upper level to the ground in all directions, like giant tent ropes. 'The colonel is out there overseeing the raising of our felled fighting machine. He has an elaborate plan that he is anxious to put to good use. He'll be in as soon as the machine is hoisted up. In the meantime, we can go to the hospital tank and prepare for the meeting to come.'

'That sounds like an excellent plan, Lieutenant,' agreed Dr Cheema. 'It will give Miss Clairmont and I a chance to freshen up.'

'Indeed, it would,' agreed Paige as he made his way down the main ladder to the bottom of the huge tank where Curtis was still at his desk, checking maps and other written coordinates.

Miss Clairmont came down the ladder next, with the doctor following. Lieutenant Paige stood back and indicated for Miss Clairmont to enter the pipe system first. He allowed Dr Cheema to go next and then followed them, heading towards their makeshift hospital-cum-conference room.

Above, in the observation gantry, Wickham and Parker looked down enviously.

'How the other half live,' said Wickham.

'I'd love to be at that little meeting,' added Parker. 'I bet there'll be all sorts of interesting snippets of information, especially about things that can kill Martians. Suddenly, the blooming hideous things don't look so superior. They can die and we can kill them a little better than before.'

For around twenty minutes, Wickham and Parker looked out over the lake. They enjoyed the enthusiastic endeavours of the Wake Men engineers. A rare sunny day with ever growing feelings of optimism. They were all deep inside Martian-dominated territory but were walking around with an air of freedom, secure in the knowledge of their deviously concealed complex. The only fighting machines in sight remained the two destroyed vessels lying in the lake water. Their Martian occupants were now dissected specimens on Dr Cheema and Miss Clairmont's operating slab.

Both observer soldiers watched with interest as Wake Men engineers clambered over one of the wrecked fighting machines. They continued to fasten more ropes around various parts of the huge contraption and then stood back as the tethers went taut, up through the rigs' various creaking pulley systems.

'Not wasting much time, are they?' muttered Parker with a note of awe.

'They'll want to raise that wrecked fighting machine as soon as possible. Quick preparation is needed. All those pulley systems on top of each scaffold are meant to lift that great contraption. I'm surprised those winches can hold such weight,' exclaimed Wickham, pointing out of the observation slit.

'There are several of them,' Parker answered. 'The weight is being evenly distributed around each tower. It looks like a crane or hoist. I think they have them at the docks, or something like them.'

'But the two towers must bear the brunt of the weight! Even half the demand for each scaffold seems like a very big ask.' Wickham wiped the sweat from beneath his pith helmet with his grubby handkerchief.

'I wonder what all this is in aid of,' said Parker, sighing.

'Another lure for another fighting machine?' Wickham frowned. 'I think our colonel is working on bringing the fighting machines to us, over land of our choosing with manoeuvrable underwater mines and all. We can strike them while being hidden. They could be fooled by a fighting machine too. How would they know we have control of such a machine?'

Parker gasped. 'I don't like the sound of that. I think we were fortunate during that last encounter. We hit two fighting machines hard and fast with our Wake Men doing a great mop-up job on the Martians inside the vessels. Our captured heat ray devices worked well too. I'm not so keen on a repeat performance. Sooner or later our luck must run out.'

'Maybe Martian luck has run out,' countered Wickham. 'Sooner or later, for better or worse, we have to confront these creatures from Mars. This way has allowed us to bring down the creatures, and our own scientists have discovered encouraging things too. Until a better way comes along, we must work with what we've got. Right now, the colonel's methods have delivered. They have opened doors for Dr Cheema and his assistant too. Who knows where all of this can lead? I can't help feeling encouraged by all of this set-up and our new-found ability to confront the Martians. It's a blinking sight better than hiding all the time.'

Parker moved forward and put his face to the opening. Then he reluctantly conceded, 'It might fool another Martian. I won't hold my breath though.'

'There's the old boy now.' Wickham pointed towards the old soldier in immaculate khaki beige trousers and khaki green jacket, supplemented by a clean beige pith helmet. The high-ranking officer had a big drooping white moustache and a walking cane.

'The old colonel seems to be an industrious man,' Parker replied, nodding while he watched through the spy slit.

Colonel Blake was pointing up at the rigging while conversing with another unknown major wearing a khaki beige jacket.

'Why do upper-ranking officers always seem to enjoy indulging themselves with an odd contrast of uniform?' Wickham sniggered.

'They do enjoy that little odd contrast of kit,' agreed Parker.

'I think they have their own little tolerated fashions.' Wickham chuckled once more.

'Could you imagine the uproar if any of us tried to do the odd little contrasting look?'

Again, Wickham giggled at the thought. 'God love us! Our feet wouldn't touch the ground before being frogmarched off.'

'Each of those officers has no waders,' Parker added.

'They don't need them. They're standing on one of the rafts with two Wake Men punting them wherever they want. Ole Hereward will have his punters bring them here soon.'

'How do you know that?' Parker seemed perplexed.

'The two officers will need to be briefed on Dr Cheema and Miss Clairmont's findings. Lieutenant Paige seems to think so, anyway,' replied Wickham. 'I bet the top brass get brought right up to the conning tower on the raft. They'll be able to climb in via the slanting gantry link.'

'How the other half live,' said Parker sarcastically.

'If the Martians are dying of disease, you might wonder why we are continuing to do all of this battle-ready preparation work?' Wickham twitched his nose and smiled indulgently.

'We don't know if all of the Martians are dying of blight and stuff.' Parker sighed. 'It's a nice thought, but perhaps a big ask of the Almighty.'

'I would have thought the Almighty might have thrown us a bone.'

'Well, God may have done just that, but we're not that sure just yet. Then the fighting machine under our new management makes sense. Probably worth a try.' Now, Parker was finding reasons to confront the alien invasion with man-made weapons and adaptation.

Wickham nodded. 'After last night, I would agree. But we lured them into the trap. This new tripod of ours has to be another well-developed trap. It will need to be a blooming good one too.'

Parker began to laugh and pointed through the slit. 'Oh my God! I don't believe it. Take a look at that.'

Wickham smiled. 'I think that looks bloody champion.'

They watched as a grubby and frayed Union Jack was fixed to the side of the Martian fighting machine's hull. Beneath it was a Wake Man, balanced on some rigging, painting a name in thick black letters. It said 'Hereward'.

'Look at the colonel,' added Parker.

'He's loving it,' agreed Wickham.

Both men watched in delight as the smiling colonel chuckled to the major, pointing his walking cane up at the wording and the worn British flag.

'Everyone loves a dab of patriotism,' said Wickham.

'I don't mind watching it from a safe distance,' replied Parker cynically.

'I think the colonel is beckoning for the raft punters,' added Wickham.

'Do you think he'll come here?'

'Well, Parker. Lieutenant Paige seems to think Colonel Blake wants to see Dr Cheema and his assistant, as I just mentioned. So, I would presume he does want to come across to this little lookout tower of ours.'

At that very moment, Lieutenant Paige's voice was heard conversing with Sergeant Curtis concerning other observation posts. He looked up at the men on the gantry and smiled when he noticed Wickham staring down.

'What is it, Corporal?' asked Paige.

'I think the colonel is being brought over the lake towards our tower, Sir,' Wickham informed him.

'Very good, Corporal,' said Paige as he started to climb the ladder. 'That is splendid timing as Dr Cheema and Miss Clairmont are preparing their notes in readiness. They have almost finished freshening up and are eager to inform the colonel of their recent findings.'

Paige went up the smaller secondary ladder to lift the conning tower hatch. The raft carrying the colonel and a major was making its way to the sloping gantry. The commanding officer wore a stern look above a bushy white drooping moustache. He seemed like a quintessential British army officer of Queen Victoria's army. There the colonel stood, on the moving raft with his walking stick slowly slapping against his knee-high riding boots.

Parker whispered again, to himself in disbelief, while looking through the spy slit. 'No waders like the rest of the Wake Men.'

'No,' agreed Wickham. 'But keep the disapproval to yourself.'

'Should I?' whispered Parker sarcastically. 'And there was me, a low-ranking private, getting ready to tear the colonel off a strip on the matter.'

'The colonel and the major don't need them at the moment,' hissed Wickham beneath his breath.

'Not planning on doing outdoor fighting then?' whispered Parker, careful not to let Paige overhear him.

'Now, now, Parker.' Wickham quietly rebuked his subordinate companion and then pointed his finger warningly at the man's nose. 'Behave, lad!'

Lieutenant Paige had climbed out onto the gantry platform. He stood to attention and saluted the oncoming raft. Colonel Blake straightened and returned the salute.

Colonel Blake then continued to gently slap the walking stick against his boot. 'The next part of our ambitious mission is being prepared, Lieutenant Paige. All this thanks to the valuable contribution your observation post put in last night. A dashed good show. A dashed good show, indeed.'

The punters stopped the raft beside the conning tower, allowing the two officers to climb aboard the ramp and then up and into the conning tower hatch. Lieutenant Paige then lifted the platform off its hooks and lowered the gantry below the surface of the lake water. Once this was complete, he followed the colonel and the accompanying major up the outer rungs, while cursing the red weed beneath his breath. All quickly clambered inside the conning tower hatch and then Paige closed the trapdoor behind them.

By the time Paige had stepped onto the observation gantry, Corporal Wickham and Private Parker were looking confused, and they nodded towards the main ladder leading down to the bottom of the submerged tank, both men indicating that the colonel and the major had descended further down. Surprised at the nimbleness of the two senior officers, Paige frowned and went after them. He noticed Sergeant Curtis quickly putting on his pith helmet and standing to salute the two senior officers.

'As you were, Sergeant. Carry on, carry on, old boy. Doing a grand job.' The colonel's voice boomed with satisfaction.

'Yes, Sir – thank you, Sir,' he replied and sat down.

The colonel looked up to see Lieutenant Paige coming down the main ladder. 'Well, Lieutenant Paige, you lead the way, old chap, there's a good fellow.'

'Yes, Sir,' Paige replied.

All the officers disappeared into the piping system, bent over double, their footsteps receding as they moved towards the second submerged tank room – the hospital area that had no wounded so far. The few that had been hit by heat ray could never tell their story. They were dead in the lake.

Back up on the gantry, Parker looked down and muttered, 'I'd like to be a fly on the wall for that little chat. I wonder what the colonel will think of Dr Cheema and Miss Clairmont's discovery? Oh, if we could just stay put and keep quiet, watch the Martians die in their own sweet way. It would be wonderfully simple. But we can never be sure the vermin creatures are all going to die.'

Wickham nodded. 'Sadly this is so, we only have the Martians that Dr Cheema and Miss Clairmont have examined. It's no good us speculating over it all again. I doubt if Colonel Blake would put all his eggs in the disease basket. He's a soldier in charge of soldiers. He has been successful with his Wake Men Militia. If he continues to confront Martians that are already dying, it could be a double attack.

Germs and soldiers that have developed a way of fighting them – a two-sided attack instead of one. How many people could the Martians kill before the diseases begin to take a toll? I doubt if the colonel can rest on such laurels.'

'He seems like a rather cheerful fellow. Responsibility doesn't faze him one bit,' said Parker with a twinge of begrudging admiration.

'The world is full of armchair sceptics. We all love to slate people in authority. Bemoan about them not knowing what they're doing, and expecting them to lead in the way we would fantasise about doing things. The truth is—'

'We wouldn't be inclined to do anything better in the first place,' Parker cut in. 'I think the army does teach us things like that. Criticism is easy and cheap when a bloke's backside is in an armchair. We're all world-beaters then, while riding through our little inebriated thoughts. Getting up and doing a better job is probably a whole new ball game. I wouldn't want that responsibility. I'd sooner be here watching through these little spy holes with some route of escape if something goes wrong.'

Wickham looked impressed. He raised an eyebrow admiringly. 'Well, Parker! I'm blown over by your little critical rant. I'm amazed it's not aimed at the top brass, but instead, at our own class. I would never have thought this of you.'

'Well,' Parker admitted reluctantly. 'The old colonel does seem the type of toff most of us like to mock. But let's be honest, the old boy did get this pipework system done in quick time. He solved so many things.'

'He had others helping him,' answered Wickham. 'He didn't do it on his own.'

'Agreed, but the colonel knew who to bring in and how to organise it all. He also knew what he was doing with the underwater bomb devices. He had the foresight to make it happen. All these educated people combined are getting towards some sort of answer. It seems to be a hook or by crook thing, but somehow, something is getting done right.'

'Yes, I can appreciate that. Dr Cheema and Miss Clairmont with their university educations all make for little movements in the right direction. Now we're looking at two ways Martians can die – tricking them to walk onto booby traps and Earthly diseases.'

'Yes,' Parker agreed. 'The booby traps are a very good way, but we need the right type of layout. The flooded fen for instance. It's small and focuses on a minor number of fighting machines. What Dr Cheema and Miss Clairmont have discovered is a much broader thing.'

Wickham nodded and smiled. 'I think there is a God. And I'm trusting he is on our side.'

'Surely God made Martians too?' added Parker, returning to his more cynical outlook.

'Well, of course God did. But seeing as this planet is ours, I'm rather banking on the Almighty cheering for us.' Wickham chuckled humorously.

Parker smiled too. It was a light-hearted way of passing the time with a bit of banter. 'My old dad used to say, "God helps those who help themselves." Hopefully, Colonel Blake, Dr Cheema and Miss Clairmont fall into that group.'

'Well, look at that!' Wickham gulped in astonishment as he pointed to the spy slit.

Parker frowned and then also gasped with awe. 'Blooming heck! They're doing it. Colonel Blake is showing us his way of God helping those who help themselves.'

Wickham nodded. 'So, Colonel Blake hopes to help himself to some more Martian fighting machines with this new resurrected British fighting machine. This *Hereward* – an adaptation of our own?'

'Oh, my word!' Parker's interest was suddenly captured as his eyes bulged, looking out of the observation slit.

The two soldiers indulged in sharp intakes of breath and little whistles of appreciation. Before them, an unfolding vision of wonder. The derelict tripod and the rigged tackle began to creak – taut ropes, hoists and winches, straining under immense pressure. The sight of an almost heavenly, yet demanding task. Then, both men were struck dumb, each holding his breath to the seduction of a truly magnificent sight. They witnessed the slow rise of the *Hereward.*

Some of the Wake Men engineers seemed to be bracing themselves for the expected fall, the imagined catastrophe of thick ropes snapping or the scaffold towers collapsing. Thankfully, it never happened. The makeshift cranes stood firm, much to the surprise of all the onlookers. Gradually, the fighting machine's alien capsule continued its ambitious ascent. Foot by foot, the cabin climbed into the Fenland's clear summer afternoon, like a giant metallic wasp, slowly taking off and stopping to momentarily hover. Then, further heaving continued. Two of the three legs remained attached to the trunk, the useless appendages dragged up with the cabin, mud and filthy water cascading down. It poured from various panel tributaries and the strange redundant leg joints. Vulgar waterfalls from the defeated yet imposing monument of extra-terrestrial technology. Bit by bit, the giant sentinel attained its full potential. There were handshakes and whistles of achievement from the Wake Men engineers – an infectious glee as satisfaction flooded all the human beholders.

Parker turned and grinned to his companion. 'Our own fighting machine standing tall and waiting for Martians to come forth. I like our worn and muddy Union Jack. It looks like it's been ironed on against that strange Martian metal.'

CHAPTER 11

AHEAD WITH THE NEXT ATTACK PLAN

Lieutenant Paige arrived back in the observation tank area after about an hour. The colonel and his major had moved on via the tunnel system. Their headquarters were deeper into the flooded fen – a nerve centre from where everything was controlled. He had a brief word with Sergeant Curtis and then looked up to his faithful observation crew, sitting on the raised gantry.

'Any developments, Corporal?' Paige asked enthusiastically.

'The wrecked fighting machine has been raised, Sir,' Wickham replied and then added, 'They've even re-attached the leg by a crude method of tethering. The one that was ripped off during the battle. It looks like a bit of a messy job, Sir. But at a distance and at night, I doubt any Martian fighting machine will notice until right up close.'

Parker was also keen to alert the lieutenant to certain developments. 'They've also built a small platform to the side of the raised machine's trunk, Sir. Just below our flag and where the name "Hereward" has been painted. They've set up one of the severed heat ray guns there, Sir. A special crew, who know how to fire the Martian weapon, is now on standby on the platform.'

'Excellent,' said Paige as he immediately climbed the ladder to look through the spy slit.

'It's just out there, Sir, and we have a very good view of the whole thing,' added Wickham as he stood aside.

Paige decided that he had no need of binoculars. The event outside was very close. He bent forward to look through the spy hole and whistled like a commoner, perhaps indulging the chaps around him. 'I must say, that is an incredible sight. Colonel Blake said as much. Do you know what he wants to do?'

'Use it against the Martians, Sir?' replied Parker.

'Indeed, he does. We can't work the perishing thing, it's too badly wrecked. Plus, we do not understand the complicated control system inside the cubicle area where the Martians worked the machine. But we do know how to use the heat ray device and we are confident we can trick the next Martian fighting machine into wading across the lake towards our *Hereward* fighting machine.'

'You mean to just make the Martian machine come to us, Sir?' asked Wickham. 'I thought we were going to lure another machine in some way, but I'm not sure how this *Hereward* plan will work out.'

'I've been told of a rudimentary plan. It is almost the same as the first, which netted two fighting machines for us,' Lieutenant Paige began. 'We are to use the firework lure once again, but this time our *Hereward* fighting machine will be firing at the island and we'll create the illusion of artillery and bullets firing back at the *Hereward*. A fake firefight between an embattled fighting machine and human foes. This, in turn, will prompt a real Martian fighting machine to come to our aid. We'll use the same underwater mining opportunities as before. If this works again, then fine. But there could be more than one machine to deal with. That huge four-piloted machine could come back – Colonel Blake seems to think it is a distinct possibility. Then hopefully, we could let it come in close to aid our fake conflict, before turning the *Hereward*'s heat ray device on the big Martian war machine – at point-blank range.'

Parker's face went white with sheer fright, the colour draining from his cheeks. 'Do you think it'll work, Sir?'

'Well, I hope so, Parker. I'm going to be in the *Hereward* with Colonel Blake. He insists on being in the fighting machine too. Dr Cheema, Miss Clairmont, Major Munro and I tried to persuade the colonel not to do this, but his mind is made up. Major Munro will head the operation from the headquarters bunker, while the colonel and I with some Wake Men engineers, will oversee the facade of luring our next Martian guest.'

'What will we be doing, Sir?' asked Parker, looking very nervous indeed.

'The same as usual, Parker. You and Corporal Wickham are doing a sound job in observation. You'll call down any necessary developments to Sergeant Curtis and he can telegraph or telephone Headquarters. Plain and simple, but crucial. Are you up to it, young Parker?'

Parker smiled as relief crossed his face. His cheeks began to redden. 'Yes, Sir. We are up to the job.'

'Sound men – you and Corporal Wickham.'

Wickham spoke with a note of concern in his voice. 'Sir, you'll be careful in the *Hereward*. The machine will quickly become a target if there is more than one fighting machine lured in. I think the *Hereward* could strike a blow for us at close range, but it might be a short-lived victory if other fighting machines realise what's going on. They'll turn their heat rays on the *Hereward* very quickly.'

'This is so, Wickham, but we're fighting a war and unfortunately soldiers must risk an enemy firing back. We must all play our part in this. The colonel wants to be in on this dangerous task too.'

'Hopefully more Martians for Dr Cheema and Miss Clairmont to dissect?' added Parker.

'Dr Cheema and Miss Clairmont are hoping our Wake Men ground forces will capture one of these Martian blighters alive. When the next lot of Wake Men go into the poisonous black smoke from a downed machine, Dr Cheema and Miss Clairmont have requested the opportunity to follow the Wake Men advance into the smoke. They, like Colonel Blake, also seemed very insistent. I think they have ambitions of carving up one of these Martians, while it's still alive. I can't think of any other reason why they would want a live specimen. I would normally think such a thing rather ghastly, but somehow, I can't bring myself to feel sympathetic to such a Martian's unlucky fate. Not after all that blood-sucking they've been doing to humanity. Remember, the blighters have been feeding off us.'

'Maybe Dr Cheema can learn other things,' replied Wickham.

'Where is Dr Cheema and Miss Clairmont now, Sir?'

'Under blankets and, each one, asleep on a chosen operating table, I think. Remember, they have been dissecting Martians all night and much of the day, and writing important notes from their many discoveries. I think they were rather exhausted after the meeting with Colonel Blake. They'll be refreshed after some sleep. Have you chaps managed to get some sleep?'

'Yes, Sir,' replied Wickham. 'Small spells here and there. Used the ablution along the piping system too.'

All turned their attention to the ongoing preparations outside. The clear blue sky was still spreading its aura of delight over the flood lake and the Wake Men were still busy working on various projects. Some were setting up fireworks for the facade to come. Others were up around the raised fighting machine with its Union Jack plastered across the side of the strange alloy. The small makeshift balcony, Parker spoke of, supported a group of three Wake Men. They worked on bolting their heat ray device – a Martian gun that could swing and turn in a variety of directions.

Above the machine's trunk, the pulley systems upon the tower scaffolds could also slowly turn the huge cabin a little more, where the Martian crew once operated the machine. It was not a great degree of turn, but enough for about twenty degrees either way. At close quarters, it would be all the swing needed.

'So, the whole thing just basically stands still on the spot with a little play from side to side and up and down,' said Parker.

'That is so. The Martian-controlled machines will have to walk in front of the heat ray's sight. Then we can let the hostile Martian machine have a taste of its own medicine,' replied Lieutenant Paige.

Wickham smiled. 'The strange thing is, I think the Martians might do just that. It's a simple plan, but then sometimes simple plans work.'

'I can see it working once, but I can also believe other fighting machines will spot the trick and quickly turn on the *Hereward*,' Parker said, adding his opinion.

'Don't forget that the other fighting machines might also be trying to walk the flooded fen too,' replied Wickham. 'A lake full of ready-made underwater mines that we can slide in front of the approaching fighting machines. It might turn out to be another big shoot-out like yesterday's battle.'

'I suppose we could all live with that if the end result is the same.' Parker chuckled at the thought.

Lieutenant Paige smiled. 'That's the spirit. The result must be for our chaps. I like that, Parker. Keep your chin up, young man. After all, we're beginning to see a hopeful light at the end of a dark tunnel.'

Another three hours passed as the observation unit quietly indulged in watching the work upon the raised *Hereward* and the firework island preparations. They all cheered up when they heard the awkward push of the canteen trolly. It squeaked intolerably as it came along the pipe system. For the soldiers on duty, it was a grand sound but for the old Salvation Army tea lady it was almost insufferable. The dour old woman entered the tank, bringing with her sandwiches and heated tea urn.

Each soldier looked delighted, but the old lady was in a foul mood. She always was. The trolly kept squeaking and the soldiers liked to hear it squeaking. She hated it for the obvious reason.

'We love the sound of that,' said Sergeant Curtis, getting up from his desk and going towards the old lady.

'You don't have to put up with the blooming thing for hours on end while walking these blooming pipes, do you?' replied the old tea lady in her usual banal voice. 'We got some milk and sugar today and there are corn beef and tomato sandwiches, plus cheese and tomato too.'

'Splendid,' Paige called down. 'So we are all able to enjoy a minor repast.'

'Minor is about as good as it's going to get, Sir,' said the dreary old Salvation Army lady.

'Where did they get the bread from?' Parker called down.

'We got a bakery and a lot of flour and wheat in the storage compartments now,' answered the old woman.

Parker whispered delightedly, 'She has all the attributes of an old and accepted miserable tea lady. Just like you'd get in any pen-pusher's office.'

Wickham chuckled. 'She's a wonderful piece of work, isn't she?'

Sergeant Curtis did the honours of handing up three cups of sugared tea and three wrapped sandwiches for the observers.

Parker unwrapped his sandwich and bit into the mature cheese and tomato. 'Oh, luxury!' He closed his eyes in a moment of exquisite bliss.

The old lady looked up through her round, black-rimmed spectacles. Her wrinkled, severe face was complemented by a neat red scarf beneath her chin and a smart Salvation Army hat resting slightly sideways upon her grey hair. 'Well, he seems to like the bread.' There was a note of satisfaction in her voice.

'Well, this one has been kept on a back boiler. Nice thick doorsteps too,' added Wickham, equally pleased as he opened his wrapping to look eagerly at his corn beef and tomato sandwich.

'We've only been going a day,' said the miserable old Salvation Army lady. 'It's something that's just started.'

Wickham smiled down awkwardly. 'Well, it is greatly appreciated, madam.'

'You be welcome,' she replied and pushed her trolly on into the next section of piping towards the next observation post.

'Her trolly squeaking towards an eagerly awaiting Observation Post Eight,' Sergeant Curtis tittered as he returned to his desk.

'I don't think she gets invited to many parties,' said Parker.

Lieutenant Paige laughed as he bit into his sandwich. 'You might have a point there, Parker. But right now, she has to be my favourite miserable old and wrinkled lady.'

Wickham sniggered in agreement. 'Mine too, Sir. I could suffer her all day long with that squeaky trolly and miserable expression. Just so long as she brings hot tea and sandwiches.'

'As miserable old ladies go,' added Private Parker, after swallowing a pleasant chunk of bread and cheese. 'I think she takes the biscuit.'

The minor amusement was suddenly broken when the telephone rang down in the tank, where Sergeant Curtis sat working across his maps and gulping down a chunk of cheese and tomato sandwich. He quickly picked up the receiver.

'Yes, Sir. The lieutenant is above in the gantry, Sir,' Curtis said into the telephone receiver. 'I will, Sir – immediately.' He put the phone down and looked up at Paige, who was watching expectantly.

'Good news I hope, Sergeant Curtis?'

'A development, Sir,' answered Curtis. 'First, Colonel Blake will soon be coming across the lake on another raft. He wants to go aboard the

Hereward. He also wants you to go there too, Sir. Secondly, Headquarters has got a telegram message from Spalding in Lincolnshire. The four-crew Martian fighting machine and two other standard double-crewed machines are moving in the direction of Wisbech. I think that is too early, Sir. There is still a lot of daylight and the confrontation would be preferred at night.'

'About another hour before dusk, Sir,' said Wickham.

Paige took another bite of his sandwich and a gulp of tea before going up to the exit hatch and opening it. He climbed out into the summer day and called to the working Wake Men.

'Martian activity possibly coming this way,' he said. 'Report in from Spalding.'

All stopped working and looked to their respective men in charge of the groups. Shouts of command ensued, and all Wake Men hurried onto the waiting rafts. In a matter of minutes, they were all being ferried away from the observation post and the raised *Hereward* static fighting machine. An eerie silence fell upon the place.

'The tripods will be here easily before nightfall, Sir,' said Wickham, who had raised his head out of the conning tower exit hatch.

'Yes, that does pose a problem,' agreed Paige. He looked up at the suspended capsule of the *Hereward* and noted the crew of the captured heat ray gun were still manning their position.

'One moment, Sir. I think Sergeant Curtis has had another phone call.' Wickham disappeared back inside the shelter. He was gone for a few moments before re-emerging with new information. 'The sergeant has been informed on the telephone by Major Munro, Sir. A firework diversion around the abandoned town of Holbeach, designed to make the fighting machines explore the source of the noise. Might keep them preoccupied until dusk.'

'Well, that is something that could buy us some time, Corporal. I think you should go inside and close the hatch. I'm going to get aboard the *Hereward* and wait for Colonel Blake.'

'Very good, Sir.' Wickham closed the hatch lid without further instruction.

Immediately, one of the Wake Men called down from *Hereward*'s makeshift gun platform. 'The colonel's raft has been spotted, Sir.'

'Very good, drop me a ladder, man. I'm coming up now,' called Paige as he once again lifted the gantry up out of the flood water and hooked it to the side grips. He then made his way down the walkway into the lake water and began to wade towards the *Hereward*. The true test was about to begin.

CHAPTER 12

THE ECCENTRIC COLONEL BLAKE

Colonel Blake waded through the still waters towards the dark edifice that was the *Hereward*. Lieutenant Paige followed. No one dared to carry a light. Only the dark silhouette of the raised and tethered fighting machine could be made out – its ominous outline a vague spectre in the mildly illuminated night sky.

'Didn't need to come down from the *Hereward* to meet me, Lieutenant. Kind of you, old chap, but not necessary.' The colonel was light-hearted with his mild rebuke.

Lieutenant Paige smiled. Even the colonel's chest waders were different in colour from every other Wake Man. His were beige as opposed to green. 'Wasn't sure you might see us in the night, Sir. Thought it better to come down and guide you when the raft stopped at the gantry platform.'

'Have you managed to climb inside the control room of the machine, Lieutenant?'

'Not yet, Sir. I stayed on the platform with the gun crew. I've spoken to Sergeant Ruddock via a short wire link on the platform. He's exploring the inside of the control room. Much of it is burnt out by our shell strike.'

'The night is very different from the clear sunny day we've had, Lieutenant Paige,' said the colonel, changing the subject. They moved through the gently lapping water, closer to the giant apparition.

Paige replied, 'The breeze coupled with this light rain adds to a sombre and dark mood, Sir.'

The colonel chuckled. 'I say, aren't we typical British chaps. Here we are in the most frightful predicament with Martians from another planet. An actual War of the Worlds, you know. And yet, we still find time to berate the weather.' He grabbed the strap on his chest waders, checking the hold upon his shoulder.

Paige nodded. After all, the old colonel was correct. 'Well, Sir, we mustn't let standards slip.' He followed through the colonel's dispersing murky backwash, the placid sloshing inspiring the gloomy ambiance of the night.

'I know what you mean, Lieutenant. I had to laugh when I first saw that old tea lady coming along the pipes with her tea trolly. What a splendid little dear she is. Poor old biddy doesn't seem to be too troubled by the Martian invasion. Just as long as we continue to drink her tea,' Colonel Blake said with keen spirit.

'It's little things like that that keeps one ticking along, Sir. The old biddy is a very lovely lady indeed.'

'Hear, hear, Lieutenant. Good citizens like the tea lady can't be forgotten in all of this. They are the necessary people that are part of the foundation – the substance of our well-organised resistance.'

'Indeed, Sir. Corned beef sandwiches and cups of tea. Can't beat it, Sir.'

Colonel Blake halted for a moment and looked north. 'There's that distant glow on the northern horizon.'

Paige nodded. 'The Martian front line is further away now. Only the fighting machines mopping up pockets of resistance will be patrolling.'

The old colonel resumed his wading to the *Hereward* and replied, 'Here, we have a subdued Martian menace. That will still be very problematic, should their ghastly patrols come this way again. And there is every reason to suppose they will, despite not spotting far-off fighting machines at the moment. We Wake Men are, after all, a pocket of resistance. Maybe the Martians do not quite appreciate the fact yet, but they soon will.'

'They will no doubt see our resurrected Martian machine, not realising it's under human control, standing in the lake?'

'I'm banking on that prospect, Lieutenant. Hopefully they'll become inquisitive and approach our armed fighting machine unaware of the reception we have prepared.'

Paige looked up at the dark titan as they got closer. 'The *Hereward* fighting machine – our dark sentinel that seems unsure of its purpose.'

Again, the colonel paused and said, 'There it stands with its thick support ropes leading to those obscure scaffold towers either side.'

Paige drew level and stopped next to the old colonel. 'The machine looks as though it's standing upon its three legs, but is, in fact, hanging there with three useless limbs, looking sturdier than the broken mechanical limbs really are. The whole structure is nothing more than an illusion.'

'A deception that can fire a heat ray – trickery that can deceive another Martian machine,' added the colonel enthusiastically as he resumed his wading journey to the *Hereward*.

Lieutenant Paige smiled after the colonel. He was a very remarkable man, an old rogue of quality. He used the world about him and searched for all sorts of tools, including devious and cheating methods. 'Any trick in the book will do,' Paige muttered to himself in awe.

They got closer and looked up again to the raised capsule that was once occupied by the Martians. They were underneath the small hastily assembled platform that was to one side.

Paige gripped the ladder and tested its sturdiness. 'Firmly fixed leading up to a small halfway platform, Sir.'

'Yes, halfway up the tripod's leg. Looks like a swollen kneecap,' said Colonel Blake, chuckling. 'And from this small platform, I see they've fixed a second ladder that goes up to the bigger gun platform at the side of the cubicle section. I must presume you have already had a good look about from the gun platform we put in?'

'I did, Sir. A grand view of the fen. As I recently said, I've not had time to look inside the capsule. Just the gun platform where I got acquainted with the crew of our captured heat ray device. The work was all but done and the Wake Men were testing the swivel that holds the Martian weapon. A good idea to hold the device firmly on the railings,' said Lieutenant Paige. He followed the colonel's ascent of the ladder and now emerged onto the first upper position. The colonel had waited for him and was looking north again at the glowing horizon.

Paige tipped the gas mask that hung about his neck on its side and let the collected drizzle run out. He did not approve of the breeze or the irritating light rain.

'Very good, indeed,' Colonel Blake said with a big beaming smile.

The old soldier seemed invigorated by the rain and breeze as he began to climb the second ladder leading to the higher gun platform. As he reached the top to stand upon the final balcony, he looked to the gun crew. All of them had stopped and stood to attention before saluting, the drizzle running down off the surrounding rim of the men's pith helmets.

'Carry on, men. Take no notice of us. We are going to enter the contraption. We want to see if we can get the blithering Martian service hatch to work from inside of this control section. Hard to understand the inner workings of this craft, I'm told.'

'Sergeant Ruddock is inside trying to fathom it out, Sir. He seems to think the shot that smashed through the green window thing destroyed much of the inner workings. We have managed to connect a telephone wire down one of the legs and across the lake to OP Nine, Sir,' a young corporal politely replied.

Again, Colonel Blake smiled. 'Sound fellows. Sound fellows, indeed.' He meant every word of what he said. He was very proud of his Wake Men. The old man looked about the balcony in wonder. He was overjoyed by the adaptation of his men. 'These little shows of initiative are first class, men. I was thinking of us mounting the heat ray device inside that burnt-out cabin, but this is a splendid innovation. This safeguard rail that you fellows have constructed around our upper gun platform, it's first class. Our very own *Hereward* gunnery team.'

'Thank you, Sir,' the three soldiers replied in unison. They were uplifted by the praise and gratified by the true intention of Colonel Blake's fine words.

'Right then,' the colonel continued as he looked to Lieutenant Paige. The young officer was just climbing onto the platform. Blake pointed his cane at some net rigging that led around the front of the *Hereward*. 'I take it this rigging must be used to enter the cubicle via the broken green window screen. Is all that green goo still seeping from the resin-type skin?'

'No, Sir,' Paige replied, looking at the broken shards of the green visor screen's window. 'The liquid seems to have solidified around the smashed pane, almost like blood coagulation.'

'Very well, let's make our way around to the only entrance we have until we can find a way of opening the side hatch. There's one just there.' He pointed his walking cane at a panel on the side of the sloping Martian alloy.

'Yes, Sir. It would serve us well if we could find a way of opening it.'

'Let's not stand on ceremony then, Lieutenant. Off we go.' The colonel stepped away from the platform and onto the sailing ship-style rigging and began to make his way around the front, oblivious to the sheer drop, uncaring of the continuous wind and rain.

Lieutenant Paige looked at the gun crew and raised a puzzled eyebrow before following Colonel Blake along the rigging towards the smashed screen area, whereby each could enter the inner control room where Martian operators once worked.

The colonel entered the wrecked inner control room first. He saw Sergeant Ruddock look up from his endeavour. The man had been examining a burnt panel before standing to attention.

'Carry on, Sergeant. Have you discovered anything? I spoke with the gun crew outside. One chap says that all the workings are destroyed. So I presume you are looking for snippets – something of salvage. Have you found any snippets?'

'Nothing that seems to work, Sir. There are no seats around the control panel. I thought that was odd at first but then I don't suppose Martians need to sit down, Sir.'

'I'm told the three thick lower tentacle limbs that are used to slither upon, can also act as seating – a coiled mass beneath, for the bulk to rest upon. While the thinner upper appendages with the three little digit things work the same way our hands and fingers do.' He put his cane under his armpit and looked around at the burnt inner panels. 'My God, our strike made a thorough mess of this interior.'

Lieutenant Paige climbed through the window to stand beside the colonel. The concave surroundings were unsettling. The walls seemed wet with a shining surface that had vein lines beneath the confining membrane. There was a huge circular scorch mark to the back of the container. It looked like a giant dark-grey ulcer against wet skin tissue.

Colonel Blake noticed Lieutenant Paige's scrutiny. He raised his cane and pointed to the breach in the lower section of wall, just below the screen where Paige had entered the capsule. 'One can make out the trajectory of the shell entering through here.' He then turned and pointed his cane to the black ulcerated impact mark. 'And then hitting the wall at the back. The following explosion ripped through the entire interior causing all this damage.'

'Yes, Sir. What a diabolical and most extraordinary container,' Paige muttered.

'Yes,' agreed Colonel Blake. 'It's almost like we're inside some beast's mouth looking at the wet inside of the skin cheeks. All those veins beneath that wet layer of purple membrane. It's positively ghastly.'

'There is this, Sir,' said Sergeant Ruddock as he walked over to a small circular rack. 'There are others like this that have been destroyed by the internal blast.'

The colonel came forward and looked at the strange mesh of bone-like ribbing. 'It looks calcium-based. Like a ribbed horn or bone-cage construction.'

'Yes, Sir, like a cage-style cylinder. Big enough to contain a thin Martian appendage. I put a thin lever through the opening, and it lit up. Look!'

Sergeant Ruddock looked about for something thin, but the colonel beat him to the task by inserting his cane through the cylinder opening. Instantly, the inner workings lit up. He pushed at a small strand among the cage of bare strands at the end of the cylindrical device. A set of inner green lights came on over the window panel. They lasted for a few seconds before a power failure caused the glow to dim and then vanish.

'The energy that works them must be failing,' suggested Paige.

The colonel withdrew his cane and then stood upright. 'Yes. I think this is so, Lieutenant. The contraption is obviously designed to accommodate a Martian's thin arm appendage. The sergeant says there are several of them. Look! The frames are in bits over the panel. These cylinders with various threads are switches or levers. They control certain parts of this vessel. I wonder if one might open the hull door?'

'There are about forty different threads at the bottom of the cylinder. A sequence of touches might perform a different internal task. But with no power, we can hardly discover what,' Paige added.

The telephone rig set up inside the cubicle rang and Sergeant Ruddock answered it. 'The *Hereward*,' he said into the receiver and then looked to Colonel Blake. 'It's OP Nine, Sir – Sergeant Curtis.'

The colonel took the phone. After a short moment he asked, 'Are they sure these things are coming this way now. Earlier reports said they had stopped at Holbeach, that's still in Lincolnshire?'

Lieutenant Paige looked at Sergeant Ruddock. Were Martians coming again?

'Very good, Sergeant Curtis, we'll inform the gun crew,' said the colonel, then he put the phone down.

'There's a small speaking wire rigged to the outside gun crew, Sir. It's just there,' said Ruddock, pointing to the device by the broken green screen.

Colonel Blake picked it up and did the necessary to get through to the gun crew on the outside platform. As he spoke, his voice held a note of firm order. 'Three fighting machines leaving Holbeach area. Reported via Spalding observation units. Expect them to veer off, towards this position. Among the three tripods is the big unit, like the one that left the scene yesterday before we took out the two standard tripods, one of which we now occupy. Make ready for probable confrontation with the bigger of the three. We'll get one shot at this and it must count, men.' He replaced the voice pipe and looked to Paige.

The lieutenant nodded and then said, 'It seems you were correct in your assumption that the bigger fighting machine would return, Sir. We were informed earlier of movement from Spalding but the enemy patrol had stopped to investigate a diversion at Holbeach. I am presuming the Martians are on the move again.'

'This is so, Lieutenant, and I think they will eventually make their way here. And very soon. Try to look at it from a Martian perspective if we can. Two of their units go missing. Fellow Martian chums, if you like. Sooner or later, a chum's absence will cause concern for the Martians. I would expect they have some form of directional checking. In short, the Martians want to know what became of two missing fighting machines. Let's try to show them something they want to see – our *Hereward* engaged in battle against phantom humans on our firework island. Draw the big one in close and then turn the heat ray on the blighter.'

The look upon Lieutenant Paige's and Sergeant Ruddock's faces did not display a great deal of confidence.

'May the Almighty be with us.' The colonel held up his cane and grinned. He gave them an excited wink. 'This is the big one, chaps! Let's make sure our visitors get a nice warm reception.'

'Yes, Sir,' Ruddock replied.

'May the Almighty be with us. Or any other type of force we might create for ourselves,' said Paige with an unconvincing but resigned smile.

CHAPTER 13

THE BIG FIGHTING MACHINE
IS HERE

Station workers Mike and Bill came into the observation room looking very flustered. There was some sort of commotion along the tunnel where Dr Cheema and Miss Clairmont had been trying to get some sleep. They had managed about four hours, but the disturbance would have surely woken them, as it had Mike and Bill.

'What's going on?' Sergeant Curtis asked. 'Is it Wake Men getting prepared for an oncoming battle?'

Mike answered, 'That's right, Sergeant Curtis. There's loads more than last time. I think Miss Clairmont and Dr Cheema will be here soon. Can we stand up on the observation gantry with Corporal Wickham and Private Parker? I think you're going to have lots of Wake Men in here too.'

'Yes, of course you can,' replied Curtis. 'Probably the best place to be if they come in with those grasshopper men and fixed bayonets.'

The two railmen clambered up the ladder as Miss Clairmont, followed by Dr Cheema, came through the pipe opening.

Dr Cheema gasped, 'My word! It's organised chaos back there. We can't move for Wake Men and grasshopper men. Something is afoot.'

'It is, Dr Cheema,' replied Sergeant Curtis. 'It's now dusk and the delay at Holbeach has bought us the necessary time for it to get to night-time before our visitors arrive. Better to confront the Martians in the dark.'

'Holbeach? What delay?' Miss Clairmont asked in surprise as she noticed a second telephone and thick cable running up the wall to the hatchway. 'You have another telephone device,' she added.

'I certainly do, Miss Clairmont. It's a direct line to the *Hereward*, outside. Colonel Blake's insistence. I think he's rather fond of these telephone contraptions.' The sergeant smiled at her, pleased that she had noticed the new arrangement.

'Observation Post Nine seems to have been very busy while Miss Clairmont and I were resting,' Dr Cheema responded while tracing the wall line of the cable's fastening, up from the desk.

Again, Curtis smiled. 'This is so, Dr Cheema. I'll let Wickham and Parker fill you good people in on these matters. You might want to go up onto the lookout gantry with them and your rail worker assistants. The Wake Men will be spilling into here too, in a moment.'

Dr Cheema and Miss Clairmont needed no second bidding as they both climbed the ladder to stand with the familiar rail workers and the two soldiers they had come to know.

'Can you chaps inform us of any developments,' asked Dr Cheema.

'We can, Doctor,' replied Wickham. 'The colonel and Lieutenant Paige are in that resurrected tripod out there. The one we've christened the *Hereward*. They have the whole thing set up for a new project of attack. The huge four-crew and the two double-crewed Martian vehicles are coming this way from Holbeach as I speak.'

Miss Clairmont frowned as she peered out into the dusk. She could just about make out the shadow of the giant *Hereward* fighting machine. 'Is this to be the other confrontation? The one Colonel Blake wanted?'

'I think so, Miss Clairmont. The colonel, Lieutenant Paige and the heat ray crew are ready to engage the approaching fighting machines in a new battle. Mines are also being readied and dispersed within the lake approaches. All in all, a rather nasty reception committee for the Martians.'

'Well, I hope it is awfully nasty where the Martians are concerned,' said Miss Clairmont excitedly, clasping her hands together. 'I hate the vile brutes.'

Dr Cheema and all the gantry company smiled at Miss Clairmont's plucky words.

'If we're about to kill more Martians, then there's no point in beating about the bush,' agreed Parker, feeling charged with the same excitement. He was scared too, but Miss Clairmont was able to gift him with a new-found adrenalin rush. His nostrils flared with a look of complete agreement.

Below came the sound of the Wake Men as they entered, fixing their bayonets, and spreading out in several neat lines. Scattered among them were the already gasmasked grasshopper men, marker flags and pistols in readiness.

'Well, it looks as though we have ringside tickets again,' said Wickham.

'Not us,' replied Dr Cheema. 'Miss Clairmont and I will be following the Wake Men on this occasion.' He held up his gas mask.

Miss Clairmont lifted her mask too. 'We need to oversee the capture of a live Martian. Make sure the Wake Men do not bayonet one to death beforehand.'

'Suppose we don't bring one down?' asked Parker.

'Then we do not venture out, my good man,' replied Dr Cheema with a slight chuckle.

The telephone rang and Sergeant Curtis promptly answered it. Then the second telephone rang, and he quickly said, 'On the phone to HQ. With you in a second, Sir.' He went back to the HQ link and began his usual worded replies: 'Yes, Sir. Very good, Sir. Will do, Sir.' He put the main telephone down and went back to the *Hereward* line: 'Sorry for the delay, *Hereward*. Yes, HQ have said the same thing. The huge fighting machine and two standard ones following. Do you think they may be looking for the two we brought down yesterday?'

The sergeant went silent, listening to the voice at the other end of the line – a soldier, possibly the colonel himself, on board the *Hereward* fighting machine.

'We are ready and waiting, Sir,' continued Curtis. 'Wake Men and grasshopper men are all standing ready. Dr Cheema and Miss Clairmont are also ready and waiting, Sir. Very good, Sir – right away.' He put down the receiver and called out, 'Here they come!'

Miss Clairmont had been scrutinising the dark form of the *Hereward* against the night sky amid the misty rain. There remained the distant orange glow across the northern horizon. The new far-off front line – a receding tinge of humanity. She took one last look at the dull structure of the *Hereward*, its worn and frayed Union Jack plastered along the cabin's hull. Then her attention turned to the east. Spotlights approaching in the distance, belonging to the diabolical Martian machines, were sweeping to and fro.

'Wide-range searchlights getting closer,' called Wickham.

Again, the sergeant's phone rang. No one on the gantry took any notice of the conversation. They only had eyes, wide with fear, for the approaching abominations.

Curtis shouted, 'Fireworks about to commence.'

Immediately the controlled and colourful explosives of their firework island began to go off. Lights and rockets fizzed about, causing all manner of noise and flashing pandemonium. Then everyone on the gantry jumped back with shock.

The whirr of the *Hereward*'s heat ray device started up. It reached its crescendo and let loose with a high-pitched screech and a giant lance of glowing blue energy, a needle of light that shot down into firework island. An explosion followed with a second whirring charge. This time the energy seemed to spray in a sweep across the marshy island. The *Hereward* was enticing the approaching fighting machines with a fictional enemy, concealing a very real and much more deceitful human foe.

'That looks real,' said Wickham excitedly.

'Yeah,' Parker agreed. 'The approaching Martians will think one of their machines is in a firefight with our soldiers.'

'Hopefully they will.' Mike added his nervous voice to the matter.

'I think the Martians are buying it,' said Bill excitedly. He looked up at Dr Cheema and stood out of the way so the man could see for himself.

'Oh, my word, Bill. I think you're right.' The doctor watched as the huge approaching fighting machine raised one of its feelers – an appendage holding a heat ray device.

'Is it aiming at the island or the *Hereward*?' asked Miss Clairmont as she peered through the slit.

'I think it's the island, Miss Clairmont,' replied Wickham.

The whirring sound of the Martian heat ray began to charge. An energy bolt of long blue light shot forth and struck the fire-flashing island. An enormous uplift of soil and flame lit up the night further as it appeared before each observer's awe-struck gaze. They were hardly aware of the tele-phone being slammed down and Sergeant Curtis screaming, 'Underwater pendulum mines swinging towards approaching tripods!'

Instantly the spectators turned their attention to the two standard-sized fighting machines follow-ing. They were just in time to catch the first little *boom* emanating from a rising plume of water. It was next to a fighting machine's leg and the entire giant structure halted, as though the vehicle was confused. Then there followed a second *boom*. Once again, the onlookers observed a fountain of water erupt next to another of the Martian machine's legs. The entire edifice began to wobble and creak as the strange alien alloys began to grind in protest.

The companion fighting machine, next to the stricken vehicle, was compelled to stop because of the strange commotion.

'The thing looks as though it's in two minds what to do,' muttered Parker.

'The Martian operators must know this is an unexpected turn of events,' Dr Cheema agreed.

Miss Clairmont raised her hand to her mouth, not daring to say a word. She watched anxiously as the companion fighting machine lingered and scanned the stricken tripod with a green light.

Slowly the damaged machine toppled forward, the plunging machine's bulk gathering speed. All gasped as the alien vehicle crashed into the lake in a vast splattering explosion. Rolling waves in every direction. The colossal consequence of thousands of gallons of displaced water.

'Look at that!' Wickham gulped.

'The huge body mass is now immobile.' Dr Cheema was astounded.

'It's just lying there completely useless and broken.' Parker was amazed by the effect of the titan's fall.

It caused the immense escapade of the remaining fighting machines to a halt. Even the bigger leading machine came to a stop, briefly ignoring the island fireworks.

The remaining standard-sized model responded first, its bulky cabin grinding and squeaking as it bent forward to examine the stricken vessel.

Miss Clairmont was mesmerised. 'Are the Martians behind their green-tinted window screen positioning the control room to look down at their stricken associates?'

'I think you are correct, Miss Clairmont,' replied Dr Cheema in dreaded awe.

'Oh no,' exclaimed Parker. 'The huge four-crew machine has suddenly stopped too.'

'Yes,' agreed Dr Cheema. 'That thing has disengaged from its attack on the island of fireworks.'

All watched in horror as the great structure also turned its attention to the fallen fighting machine. For a moment, there was an eerie silence. The spectators just stared at the spectacle as the noise of the night breeze began to impress itself onto the scene – a vibrant night-time wind.

Then, the bigger machine shined its green probing beam down upon another wrecked fighting machine lying derelict in the lake – one of two destroyed from the previous encounter. The other was standing beside the grand alien machine. It had been engaged in the sham battle with the island of fireworks, the Union Jack fastened to the side of its trunk.

'I think the big thing has grasped that we have destroyed another fighting machine from yesterday,' added Wickham.

'I wonder if it'll realise that our *Hereward* is not on their side too?' muttered Mike.

'Oh, my word!' Miss Clairmont pointed to the crew on the makeshift balcony of the *Hereward*. 'Our boys are lining up the heat ray for a point-blank shot!'

'Blimey!' hissed Parker. 'So it is!'

There, in the night-time wind, the crew of three Wake Men toiled in their gas masks as they adjusted the heat ray device and lined the strange hollow-piped weapon up for a good shot.

'Colonel Blake and Lieutenant Paige must be inside the machine cabin,' Dr Cheema commented.

'Go on there, *Hereward*,' hissed Bill.

'Yeah, let the sod have it!' said Parker through clenched teeth.

The platform crew of Wake Men methodically set up their heat ray device into its fixed position. They wanted a good killing shot. The howling wind seemed to have little effect on the soldiers' determination. The Earthly element was covering any noise the Wake Men may have been making. The onlookers of Observation Post Nine's conning tower watched on, mesmerised by the quick preparation that seemed to be taking longer amid the rising tension each felt.

'Oh, for God's sake, please fire,' said Miss Clairmont. She could barely contain her passion.

The whirring sound started roaring through the night. The huge Martian-controlled machine turned off its green light probe that had been scanning the destroyed tripod from the previous night.

Maybe the Martians inside their colossal machine began to realise that something was wrong. What was their predicament? If the alien beings inside their machine did manage to fathom their situation, they never had time to react. The close quarters of the *Hereward* and its human-controlled heat ray were unavoidable. The huge Martian machine had walked snuggly into the trap. And, it was too late!

'Time to pay the bill,' said Parker, giggling.

The *Hereward*'s rising whirr abruptly stopped to the sound of a *woosh*. The blue javelin of light shot across the short expanse. It smashed into the green screen of the monstrous fighting machine. Grand tufts of fire erupted out from every opening and crevice the huge trunk possessed. The green visor screen to the front exploded out into the night – a giant and disgusting paroxysm of green puss that was devoured by the engulfing inferno that ensued.

The roaring flames spread around the alien booth where the Martian controllers were encased. Before the human observers was a gigantic three-legged beacon – a warning flare of all-consuming fire.

Inside the conning tower, all cheered. The joy was infectious as Parker looked down at the Wake Men and gave them a thumbs up.

'Two down – one to go,' he yelled fervently.

Dr Cheema stood upright, his tall frame dwarfing the soldiers around him. 'I don't think we'll be getting any live ones out of that contraption, Miss Clairmont.'

Miss Clairmont put her hand over her mouth and started to giggle. After all, it was rather obvious. All about the tank was further joy as the Wake Men joined in the jubilant cheering.

'I know it sounds wicked, Dr Cheema, but for the moment, I couldn't give a hoot.' She continued to chuckle.

'Good God!' said Wickham, captivated by the fireball. 'Have you ever seen such destruction.'

They returned their awestruck attention back to the magnificent sight.

Bill whistled. 'A giant Martian tripod. Still standing on three sturdy legs as its body remains that mass of all-consuming and roaring Hell.'

'Let Hell have them all,' hissed Miss Clairmont with wicked glee.

'A volcano on three skewer sticks, if there could be such a thing,' muttered Mike in admiration of the sight.

The remaining standard tripod had raised its heat ray device. None of the observers had noticed the remaining machine's new-found interest. The group was too preoccupied and spellbound by the huge fireball before them. Their attention was suddenly grabbed amid the sound of the retaliatory whirring reply.

Suddenly, the group observing within the conning tower began to call for hush to one another. All fell silent as they watched the wicked blue bolt rip out to strike the *Hereward*, the shaft of energy passing through the broken green screen into the compartment behind.

Instantly, the crash of impact boomed within the *Hereward*'s cabin. An eruption, as another rolling ball of flame emerged into the violent night, spreading more of the shattered resin's green mucus-like gunge. A feeble shriek rang out amid the torrid sound of destruction and a thrashing human torch was propelled wickedly from the fireball. A burning form arcing out into the night's robust breeze – twisting and turning as it reached maximum velocity and then arced into a downward trajectory to splash pitilessly into the lake below.

'The colonel or Lieutenant Paige?' Miss Clairmont asked in shock.

Outside, on the makeshift platform, the Wake Men with their heat ray device clung desperately onto any supports they could find. The vehicle wobbled but the prop ropes on the scaffold towers held firm. The entire fighting machine contraption was being held up like a ship's mast as it began to sway violently. The inside canopy was on fire, but the *Hereward* was not controlled from within. It was fastened up and the lines held firm.

The sway of the *Hereward* began to subside and the Wake Men on the platform commenced hurried preparation of their heat ray device.

'They're trying for a second shot,' called Parker excitedly.

'Oh, my word, I think you are correct, Private Parker,' agreed Mike.

At the same moment, all attention was diverted by the *boom* of the artillery gun on the small island to the rear of the observers' conning tower. A brief clang of metal resonated and a hole appeared in the side of the remaining Martian fighting machine's capsule.

'The thud of shell impact!' exclaimed Wickham.

'There!' Miss Clairmont pointed.

Dr Cheema called out excitedly, 'The projectile has struck its mark.'

'On the last remaining machine under Martian control,' yelled Miss Clairmont, almost jubilantly.

The small rupture momentarily appeared on the alloy casing to the side, below the green screen, the clang of striking metal still echoing in the windy night amid the various infernos.

Once again, the observers witnessed the split-second delay followed by the *boom* of an inner explosion. Another green visor screen erupted outwards and more of the vile mucus substance was discharged. A disgusting titanic sneeze quickly obscured by the emerging fireball, the cabin engulfed and quickly hidden from view. A distant heat ray shot out along the lake – a captured one from Observation Post Eight. The fighting machine's appendage was still holding the heat ray device. Its feeler, still raised above the consuming fireball, was severed instantly. The device fell into the lake to await a marker from the grasshopper men.

'Our artillery men by the lab tent,' said Dr Cheema, looking out of the other spy slit. 'They fired that artillery shot.'

'Well, it was a blooming good one, Doctor,' said Bill respectfully.

'Do you think the Wake Men will leave a live Martian for us?' said Dr Cheema with a humorous smile, briskly rubbing his hands.

Mike laughed as the disharmony of explosions continued outside. 'Would you honestly mind if they did not, Doctor?' He continued to chuckle.

'I think I could live with the disappointment, Mike,' replied the doctor. Everyone was uplifted by the commotion.

Again, the observers stared out at the flaming *Hereward* as it hung between the two supporting scaffold towers. Despite the burning condition of the captured fighting machine, the remaining crewmen on the outer balcony had managed to line up the heat ray device again. The whirring started and quickly reached its crescendo. Another blue energy bolt shot forward into the already stricken and burning Martian tripod the artillery unit had hit. This time the entire mechanism reeled backwards amid further explosions. The titan lethargically plummeted into the lake. Another huge splash and displacement of water. The entire spectacle was bathed in the light of the bigger four-crew burning tripod machine. It was still standing as it was consumed by ferocious flames – a warning that illuminated across the Fenland.

Lieutenant Paige woke up from his unconscious state and gathered his jumbled wits. How long had he been lying there?

Seconds?

Minutes?

He began to cough and splutter as he hauled himself up inside the *Hereward*'s smoke-filled cabin. There was the acrid smell of burning flesh. Not his flesh, as he looked down at his singed arms. Gingerly he felt his face. It was sore and his hair was scorched too. His pith helmet was gone, as was his gas mask. He was in a state of bewilderment and shock. One moment they had been receiving instructions from Colonel Blake, then an eruption of fantastic blue light. Was there a *woosh* that followed? Or was that his imagination? A reaction of his mind and not the blinding flash as everything went black?

He looked through the scattered smoke around the confines of the Martian control deck. Nothing major but the sporadic plumes of smoke here and there told of the recent explosive hit. The colonel was no longer at the green visor screen. What was left of the panel was now gone, including, no doubt, the late colonel. The circumstance was accepted. Colonel Blake had been blown out of the capsule. What of Sergeant Ruddock? He had briefly forgotten Sergeant Ruddock. He had been at the back of the cabin when the energy flash engulfed all.

The smouldering inner layer of the Martian capsule was hissing and bubbling away. The wall membrane's black crater was now a bigger sizzling ulcer where the heat ray's bolt had struck. The impact area contained some damning evidence of the late sergeant. A charred human skull with open mouth was imbedded in the scorched sizzling wall. Parts of the vanquished sergeant's rib cage too. It was a hideous and diabolical sight. Lieutenant Paige turned away and looked out through the opening and felt the cold night air amid the sound of continuing battle. His chest expanded as he breathed in the fresher air from outside. Refreshed as he could be under such dire circumstances, he looked out to the east.

In the distance, he made out the glowing lights of two more fighting machines approaching from the direction of Whittlesey. More trials lay ahead. The night's fighting was far from complete. Now what should he do? He was on the verge of losing his wits but began to breathe in through his nose and out via his mouth.

Consciously he followed this routine for a few seconds, then scolded himself: 'Pull yourself together, man – blast you! Others are depending on you. Act now.'

Paige got a grip of himself and noticed the telephone was inside part of the panel's alcove. It was also against the side wall and appeared to be untouched by the blast. Cautiously, he picked up the receiver and his heart jumped when he heard the whirring tone. He twisted the dial frantically, pleading: 'Please let Sergeant Curtis get this. Please, God! Do this for me.'

Again, the telephone rang, but the entire observation unit was intent on the destruction outside. It was only when Sergeant Curtis slammed the phone down, he called out, 'Two more incoming from Whittlesey. Lieutenant Paige is still alive inside the burning trunk of the *Hereward* and the phone link is still working. He informed us the Martians are making for the burning giant outside and he's getting out onto the balcony at the side of the machine.'

'There he is,' called Miss Clairmont, pointing to a dishevelled figure climbing out of the compartment wreckage and edging his way around to the platform, where the Wake Men were still manning their heat ray device.

The Wake Men instantly moved forward to aid the lieutenant and pulled him over the scaffold bulwark. All the observation group watched as the young officer began to gesticulate to the gun crew and order new instructions.

'How on Earth did the lieutenant manage to survive that hit?' Parker asked.

'Not sure, mate. But I'm very pleased he did,' replied Wickham.

They could all see that Paige was dishevelled with burnt clothing, but he continued to earnestly instruct the Wake Men on the platform.

'He's pointing towards Whittlesey,' said Mike. 'Probably telling them about the approaching tripods.'

The protest of the scaffold towers' pulley systems was heard creaking through the wind. Slowly, the *Hereward* turned towards Whittlesey, from where the approaching fighting machines would be coming.

The *Hereward* once again charged the heat ray device and the whirr ended with another blast of blue energy shooting down into the firework island. This was followed by fizzing, crackling rockets and loud bangs to give the new approaching Martians the same illusion. Could it work again?

'They're trying the same old routine,' said Parker.

'It hasn't let us down yet,' answered Wickham.

'I don't mean to be a killjoy,' said Dr Cheema, 'but there is always a first time.'

'But we'll never know that until it happens,' added Mike.

'Maybe we might get another hit before this *first time* comes?' suggested Wickham.

'I certainly hope so,' whispered Miss Clairmont as she stared through the slit at the Wake Men firing their heat ray at the fireworks on the island – a pretence of battling humans that were not concealed there. A futile something for the new approaching

Martians to focus on. Deceive the enemy by showing them something they might prefer to see.

The first machine waded into the glow of the burning Martian beacon. It was instantly greeted by a pendulum mine, the underwater swinging platform device turning towards the front leg's stride. Upon contact, there was the soft *boom* as a column of water erupted.

'Another sneaky hit,' hissed Parker excitedly through clenched teeth.

The fighting machine collapsed instantly upon the damaged leg and toppled forward like a huge unwary child tripping. Another turbulent wave of disorder fanned out across the lake. Behind, followed the second fighting machine.

The crew of the *Hereward* stopped firing at the firework island and turned their heat ray device to aim at one of the newcomers – the one that was still standing. Behind the green screen, all humans watching could make out the hazy and bulbous forms of two Martian controllers. The Martian pilots guided their tripod around the stricken fighting machine sprawled before it, the huge mechanical legs splattering through the lake water.

All attention was instantly diverted. The burning *Hereward*'s deadly whirring followed. It was a mere second but seemed like an eternity. The blue energy bolt shot across the lake to strike the oncoming

Martian machine. Its trunk erupted upon its three legs and the entire mechanism reeled.

'I don't think the blighter is going to drop,' Wickham called in concern.

'I don't think it can persevere,' added Dr Cheema.

'It's certainly wobbling,' added Bill in an almost comical manner.

'Another huge burning hulk on three giant legs that won't make it,' hissed Miss Clairmont excitedly.

'It might stay standing,' said Parker, gritting his teeth.

Miss Clairmont replied soothingly, 'Alas, no.'

The giant construction went down as a rear supporting leg collapsed. Then the entire mechanical unit toppled backwards, crashing into the shallow lake.

'This is getting too easy,' exclaimed Wickham.

'The first one that went down to the pendulum mine,' said Miss Clairmont, pointing through the slit. 'That machine is raising its heat gun. Even though it's fallen it can strike back from its injured position.'

'Good Lord!' yelled Dr Cheema.

All within the observation post inhaled fearful breaths before the dreaded sight. The first of the Whittlesey stricken fighting machines was still trying to function. One of its appendages was still holding the heat ray device. The extra-terrestrial contrivance aimed the weapon upwards, towards the *Hereward.*

The weapon began to whine for a fraction of a second before discharging another dreadful energy bolt. The *Hereward*'s burning compartment was hit for a second time. Once again, the entire trunk shook violently under the explosion. Even though the Wake Men and their gun platform was on the blind side of the strike, one of their number fell over the scaffold bulwark as the dangling machine lurched under the impact. The Wake Man fell straight down into the lake, his limbs pathetically flailing as he fell. The wretched form hit the lake back first. The smack of splattering water tearing through the night's conflict.

Parker winced. 'Crikey! That is a vicious impact.'

'I think the bloke's alright,' muttered Mike, scrutinising the scene.

To the relief of the onlookers, the Wake Man emerged to stand up. He looked battered and bruised and seemed eager to remove his water-logged chest waders. He looked back up at the crew of the burning *Hereward* and held out his arms apologetically. He called up something that was unintelligible to his onlookers.

Despite the temporary loss of a man, the burning *Hereward* still had three men with the inclusion of Lieutenant Paige. They were quickly training the sight of their heat ray down at the stricken Martian machine. The very one that had fired up at them. Another distant whirr sang out in the burning night. It came from further along the piping system.

'Observation Post Eight, again,' said Parker with a note of satisfaction.

The sweeping flash of blue-lined energy scythed through the raised appendage of the injured fighting machine and once again another heat ray device fell into the lake.

'Another for the grasshopper men,' called Mike.

In the same instance, *Hereward* fired its heat ray into the Martian canopy as it lay there, partially submerged in the lake. The explosion ripped into the inside and caused another upsurge of flame and debris.

'My word,' said Dr Cheema to Miss Clairmont. 'At this rate, I am certain there'll be no live specimens for us.'

'Oh, I think there might be, Doctor,' replied Wickham. 'Look.'

Dr Cheema nodded. 'Black poisonous smoke is emerging from two stricken fighting machines. One from the first Martian approach team via Holbeach and the other from the second Martian approach team via Whittlesey.'

'That means four potential Martians divided between two standard machines,' Miss Clairmont declared.

'Might not have two Martians live and kicking,' Parker suggested.

'Only one way to find out,' added Wickham.

Sergeant Curtis's telephone rang again. He picked up the Headquarters device and began the usual compliance of replying, 'Yes, Sir. At once, Sir. Very good, Sir.'

The phone slammed down, and Sergeant Curtis stood up. He turned to the assembled men and shouted, 'Grasshopper men move up and out into position. Wake Men follow.'

Once again, the loud yelling corporal began his usual calls to command. 'Grasshopper men first. Wake Men stand ready. Upon my command.'

The grasshopper men were instantly climbing the ladder. All gantry observers stood back to allow the men room to pass. Wickham had moved up the short-rung ladder to open the hatch. He climbed out into the night air, feeling the fresh breeze with a faint smell of the sickly red weed. Should he put his mask on? No, not yet. He heaved the rope and raised the gantry up through the water. Quickly and efficiently, Wickham hooked the rungs onto the protruding grip handles and stood back, allowing the nimble grasshopper men to make their way down the ramp and into the shallow lake. Looking like faceless clockwork figures, the strange bowler-hatted gentlemen silently descended the buoyant ramp and entered the water.

The grasshopper men congregated for a moment. One from the group pointed to various locations. Then each gasmasked man began to wade out towards the spreading black poisonous smoke, a small marker flag in one hand with pistol ready in the other.

Next, the Wake Men began to emerge from the hatch, one by one. Like the grasshopper men they descended the ramp and waded out into the water – a rifle with fixed bayonet clutched firmly in the left hand.

The loud shouting corporal had lowered his gas mask as he went down ramp, and began to call out and organise the Wake Men into a neat line. He held his fixed-bayoneted rifle up with the left hand – an example of what to copy.

'Keep your correct distance, lads,' he called as each man raised his free right hand to the next man's shoulder and spaced himself accordingly. Others coming down the ramp fell in alongside those assembled and repeated the same protocol. In a short space of time there were two neat lines of men. A few unfathomable commands came from the corporal and the Wake Men performed a rigid disciplined task that ended with them holding their fixed-bayonet rifles before them with both hands, at thirty degrees.

There were twice as many Wake Men this time around, but then there had been more fighting machines brought down. Wickham wondered if there were still enough. His attention was taken by the clatter of Dr Cheema's gas mask hitting the rim of the hatchway opening.

'Sorry, Corporal Wickham,' the doctor said.

'No problem, Dr Cheema,' replied Wickham. 'The Wake Men are getting ready to go forth.' He pulled his gas mask over his face and fastened it.

Miss Clairmont, who had already climbed out, obligingly took the doctor's Red Cross satchel.

As Wickham looked out of the lenses of his gas mask, he felt unsettled by his breathing through the ventilator at the front. He hated the rasping sound with his face confined behind the round lenses. The smell of the damp coal within the contrivance added to his discomfort. The corporal searched for a distraction and found his attention drawn to Dr Cheema's turban. It was a darker green than before. The good doctor had changed his headdress. No doubt after his rest and freshen up earlier in the day.

Miss Clairmont pulled up her mask and her humanity was replaced by an expressionless inhuman presentation. She was part of an army of apathetic insect faces – soulless figures that would confront Martians. Finally, Dr Cheema complied with his mask. One swift cloaking of facial features – withdrawing the posturing humanity that foretold his person in the world of human beholders. The dehumanised version of a man then placed the satchel straps of his first-aid kit over his shoulder.

'Be careful, Miss Clairmont and you too, Dr Cheema.' Wickham's muffled voice came from the mask – a touch of concern from something that was lifeless, his rasping breath making his manifestation all the more monstrous.

'We'll be back soon, Corporal Wickham.' Miss Clairmont smiled at the inner mould smothering her face. She wondered if the young soldier noticed her kind intention beneath the ugly gas mask.

'We shall return with a live Martian to study, Corporal.' Dr Cheema gave him a firm grip on the shoulder.

'Maybe we can learn more things about their weakness and all, Doctor. Good luck.' Wickham turned and climbed back inside the conning tower's hatch.

CHAPTER 14

THE WAKE MEN PREPARE
TO ADVANCE

'I'm not sure about Dr Cheema and Miss Clairmont following the Wake Men into the poison cloud,' said Parker as Wickham closed the conning tower hatch and removed his dreadful breathing mask.

'If I'm honest with you, Parker, I would say it is not a good idea, in my humble opinion, as well. They seem to think the Wake Men get a little over-zealous with bayoneting our Martian visitors. They want to be around to personally supervise the capture of a live one.'

'I can't understand why they don't get the Wake Men to bring them back a live one,' added Bill.

Mike scolded his friend: 'Because the Wake Men are too overenthusiastic with the bayonet! The lad just said that.'

Once again, the observer crew and the rail workers returned their scrutiny to the open spy slit. Outside in the water, the Wake Men corporal was wading back and forth along the two lines of soldiers – small waves of backwash spread from his moving person across the recently settled water, a new and milder disturbance.

'I can never make out what that corporal says.' Parker shook his head.

Wickham nodded. 'He repeats the orders given in here by the officer when they're told to assemble outside. The corporal repeats the exact words like a parrot.'

'I think he just likes the sound of his own voice,' added Bill.

'The Wake Men seem fine with him though,' replied Mike. 'At least, they seem to understand him when he's walking up and down, waffling away.'

Wickham laughed. 'I thought that too. He seems incoherent but then parade-ground holler merchants are a bit like that. I get the impression our mouthy corporal is one of your good old parade-ground holler men and his blokes know the noises even though they sound nothing like the actual intended words.'

Parker laughed too. 'They all have their own little signature, don't they? Our Wake Man corporal must take the biscuit on that front.'

Wickham chuckled on and did a quick imper-
sonation: 'Squad! Squad, shun! Squad will urn t'
height – urn height!'

'What sort of gobbledygook is that?' muttered
Mike with a raised eyebrow.

Wickham chuckled some more. 'Oh, we're
masters of gobbledygook, Mike. But I think in
honour of our corporal out there, the Wake Men
should change their name to the 1st Gobbledygook
Yeomanry.'

Bill grinned. 'That has a ring to it.'

'I like the name Wake Men,' added Mike. He
was not too up on the light-hearted banter. 'I think
Wake Men sounds better.'

The group fell silent for a moment as they let
Mike's spanner hit the works of their light-hearted
banter. Then Wickham gave them all a conciliatory
smile. 'Wake Men is indeed, a very fine name.'

'All those people deserve a hat off for recognition of bravery,' added Parker.

'Aye,' agreed Mike. 'A solid breed of soldier.'

Wickham sighed. 'They'll be going in soon and
then all Hell will break loose with heat rays, bullets and bayonets. Hideous screams – human and
Martian. A real war of the worlds hidden by black
poisonous mist.'

'I hope all of our people come out,' said Bill.

'I'm afraid that'll be unlikely, Bill.' Parker sighed.

'Lieutenant Paige and his crew are coming down the ladders of the *Hereward*,' said Wickham, pointing to the burning monument.

'The fire is getting out of control,' called Mike with concern. 'That blooming thing is going to fall. The tether ropes are burning too!'

They watched in dreadful awe as the group of men struggled down the ladder, trying to carry the dismantled heat ray device – a precious weapon that offered an advantage against the fighting machines.

Another explosion erupted out of the burning trunk and the *Hereward* wobbled more violently on its hoisting ropes. The severed leg that had been crudely fastened back in place fell away and splashed into the lake. It revealed more of the apparent dangling tripod's real condition.

'It looks pathetic like that,' Parker muttered.

'The whole thing about the *Hereward* was a charade,' added Wickham.

'A blooming good one too,' replied Mike.

'It certainly served us well,' said Parker.

'Come on, blokes!' hissed Bill, watching the soldiers struggling down the ladder with the heat ray device. 'Chuck the bloody thing in the drink. Get away before the machine goes! The grasshopper men can search for it later. That's what they do!'

Another explosion spread more debris across the lake. The assembled Wake Men watched from their bayonet-ready stance, one or two of them jumping at the sight of the falling debris.

'Stand firm, Wake Men!' called the corporal.

Dr Cheema and Miss Clairmont also looked on with dread. For a moment, the Martians in their wrecked fighting machines were of little interest. The inevitable fall of the burning *Hereward* was the main event.

'There, in the lake,' Parker called out.

'They're still clinging to that heat ray gun,' Bill hissed.

'It is a very valuable piece of equipment,' Wickham admitted.

'Lieutenant Paige is helping them,' added Parker. 'His mask is gone and he looks half blooming cooked.'

The heat ray crew of the *Hereward* quickly waded away from the fiery titan, bearing the precious Martian killing weapon. They managed to put a fair distance between themselves and the elevated swaying inferno.

'The burning support ropes attached to the two scaffold towers will soon snap,' groaned Parker.

Then, as though some divine entity was listening, one of the burning stress ropes snapped. The colossal *Hereward* jolted violently from the failure of support. A great force hit the remaining stress cables. The brutal momentum ripped through the supporting scaffold, tearing up the accompanying lines attached to stakes in the lake. One of the huge scaffold towers began to topple inwards, towards the ferocious fire of the falling giant.

The colossal noise was deafening as the huge wooden poles fell onto *Hereward*'s drenched and abating, hissing flames. Huge waves fanned out. The gun crew stopped and braced themselves for the coming wave as did the line of Wake Men. Each man jumped as the wave hit them. All were able to ride the dying surge.

'I better let them in,' said Wickham. He stood up and went to the surface hatch. Upon opening the lid, he climbed the small ladder and looked out to the lieutenant.

The rush of the open air and the sweet smell of red weed made his nostrils flare once more. Lieutenant Paige saw him and raised his hand. The rest of the gun crew, including the one who had fallen into the lake earlier, were all conversing. Heads nodded and the soldiers carrying the Martian weapon moved away from Paige and waded towards the assembled Wake Men.

'What are they doing, Sir?' Wickham called.

'They have their gas masks and want to support the Wake Men's attack. They can fire the heat ray from a holding position inside the black smoke. I can't go with them. I've lost my mask. I also need to see Sergeant Curtis. Has he reported anymore movement?'

Wickham ducked back inside the conning tower and called, 'Sergeant Curtis, Lieutenant Paige asks if there is any more movement of fighting machines?'

'Nothing coming in,' replied Curtis.

Wickham looked out of the hatch and let Lieutenant Paige know the answer to his question. He was also surprised to see the officer slowly making his way up the ramp towards the conning tower.

'Even your waders were burnt, Sir,' Wickham exclaimed.

'And leaking like Hell, Corporal Wickham,' he replied.

As he reached the conning tower, he stopped to look back at the line of Wake Men. The three men of *Hereward*'s heat ray device fell in beside the line. One either side of the weapon and one behind, aiming the contraption.

The loud corporal cleared his throat as he got ready to roar above the dying flames and the cacophony of explosions coming from the *Hereward*'s burning wreckage. He looked into the black cloud of poisonous smoke, within which were at least several more Martian machine wrecks. Many would be harbouring some live and some already dead Martians. All specimens for exploratory medical study.

The screaming order bellowed out into the burning fenland night. Uplifting and full of blind and furious confidence.

'WAKE MEN! WAKE MEN – ADVANCE!'

The first line of men proceeded with the *Hereward*'s heat ray crew fallen in beside the column. All boldly waded forward towards the nearest displacement of black fog. As the disciplined line of Wake Men went forth, they were consumed from sight by the sinister poisonous cloud. Immediately, rifle fire and heat ray screeches began to emit from the black veil. Paige could tell the louder sound of heat ray was theirs. The lighter sound of Martian hand-held weapons was also heard within the severe dispute of weaponry noise. The old corporal's orders resonated amid the discord – further alien energy weapons coupled with coordinated Earthly projectile fire. A human scream emitted from the dark obscurity. Another salvo of rifle fire followed amid freshly screamed orders. An inhuman and agonised screech of a Martian replied. The battle of the first black cloud was well under way.

Then the remaining rear line of Wake Men moved forward upon the command of the lance corporal. A second line with bayonets in readiness facing the second displacement of thick black mist.

'WAKE MEN! WAKE MEN – ADVANCE!'

The loud lance corporal walked forward with this line of Wake Men and entered the next hazy wall of fog. The same sounds followed. A salvo of gunfire followed by sporadic shots and more shouted orders. A Martian energy bolt shot out of the dark vapour across the waterlogged fen. A full-scale shooting war was going on before the observers but none could see it. Yet the noise caused them to imagine the horrors within the murky fumes.

'Bloody Hell,' muttered Wickham. 'Our blokes are going for this – big time, Sir!'

'They are, indeed, Corporal. My word, they make me proud. I think we can win this. Everything the doctor and Miss Clairmont say points to them dying and now we know we can kill the blighters too.'

Wickham nodded down at Dr Cheema and Miss Clairmont. 'They hope to get more Martians to examine. They want a live one this time. That's why they're going to follow the Wake Men in.'

'What do you mean?' Paige noticed the doctor and Miss Clairmont standing alone in the lake for the first time. All the Wake Men columns were inside the poisonous smoke clouds, indulging the Martians in battle. The lieutenant's mouth opened but no sound came out. He wanted to stop them but was just fixed to the spot. Unable to call, muffled in shock, gagged on disbelief.

Dr Cheema nodded to Miss Clairmont. Both checked their medical satchels and their masks. Then they unholstered their pistols and waded after the second line of Wake Men, following the course that the soldiers had taken – into the vociferous

black smoke where only gunfire, shouting, screaming and energy weapons emerged. The dreadful
sound ominously fanned out across the lake and
into the night.

Wickham spoke. 'I'm sorry, Sir. I thought you
knew?'

'I did know, Corporal. I honestly never believed
they would really do this. Colonel Blake never
thought they would do it either.'

'Well, they've gone into the smoke now, Sir. We
can only wait for them to emerge. Hopefully with
their live specimen.'

CHAPTER 15

THE WAY OF THINGS IN 1902

'And that was the last time I saw them,' said Sergeant Wickham to the reporters.

'By Jove!' exclaimed Humphrey Kenworthy.

'Are you saying that Dr Cheema and the good Miss Clairmont never emerged from the conflict within the ghastly black smoke?' Rupert Percival was very disappointed. He had liked the character of Miss Clairmont. He had hoped to meet her and Dr Cheema for their side of the story.

Corporal Parker sighed. 'That's the long and short of it, sadly. We never saw Miss Clairmont or the good doctor again. Only a handful of Wake Men came out of those black clouds. A few scattered survivors of the battle. They brought out a few more dead Martians to examine, but this was done by other medical people.'

Wickham continued, 'And at another location. They took the Martian corpses away on the rafts towards the deserted town of March. That's why our captain allowed us to accompany him here. This is Observation Post Nine. That tower over there, is where we watched it all happen and this drained land here, is where the lake was and where the battles took place. There are bones among the Martian wrecks. The tent yonder is where the skeletal remains are being put together by autopsy people. It was an island before the land was drained again by the Dutch engineers that are working on the embankment as we speak. Clever blokes, the Dutch. Doing a grand job, like they did centuries back. The once island is where Dr Cheema and Miss Clairmont did their pathology study on the dead Martians and discovered all the various path...path...' He struggled for the word he was looking for.

'Pathogens?' Humphrey Kenworthy ventured to add.

Sergeant Wickham held his finger up and closed one eye. 'That's the one, pathogens. They found out some very helpful things. It's difficult to say what was most important. Our small battle victories or Dr Cheema and Miss Clairmont's pathogen discoveries.'

Rupert Percival smiled and politely added, 'Well, they were all rather important to humanity, I would suppose. But long term, the discovery of Martians being partial to all manner of Earthly blight was very important. It would always happen. It would claim us the victory we needed. The Wake Men are now legendary and Dr Cheema and Miss Clairmont were forcefully conscripted into this Wake Men Militia. Therefore, as soldiers of the Wake, their discovery and the battle honours are all in the same bag of achievements, where the Wake are concerned. It is sad about Dr Cheema and his assistant. I would have dearly liked to have met them.'

'They would have been able to tell you some intricate medical things,' agreed Wickham.

'They were so excited by their discoveries and we were all heartened by this. It helped us maintain our battle-ready confidence. The sure knowledge of dying Martians and the ability to lure them into fighting on our ground and to our rules was all very uplifting.' Mike Green decided to add his own comment.

Bill Ackerman followed his work colleague and smiled. 'We were deeply saddened by the doctor's and Miss Clairmont's demise. But we'll never forget their excited banter in the lamp-lit tent, will we, Mike? They were infectious with their excited discoveries. Mike and me witnessed it all.'

'Yes,' agreed Humphrey Kenworthy. 'Mr Percival and I should like to interview you more intensely on this night of autopsy. Perhaps a little later at the local public house?'

Mike wrinkled his nose then replied, 'I'm sure it would be a pleasure, Mr Kenworthy.'

'Splendid fellows all. Your Wake Men chums are welcome too,' added Rupert Percival, looking at Sergeant Wickham and Corporal Parker.

'That would depend on our captain, Mr Percival. I'm sure he might allow it for a short time, seeing as you are reporters and all, telling the Wake Men's story.'

'Were there any further battles after the fall of the *Hereward*?' asked Kenworthy.

'A few minor intrusions,' Wickham began. 'Observation posts around Chatteris, Friday Bridge and Manea reported such things. We used the usual pendulum mines beneath the water. However, there was a noticeable drop in confrontation. Complete engagements from after our final battle with the *Hereward* never happened again. At Friday Bridge, a fighting machine collapsed after the loss of a leg to a pendulum mine. A second tripod machine that was following gripped the stricken contraption with all its appendages and pulled it away from the area. The observation crew of section fifteen watched the entire incident of this Martian machine dragging its injured companion away. The rescuing machine released shafts of heat ray bolts here, there and everywhere as it moved backwards, dragging its mate, firing blindly into the foggy lake and then laying a blanket of its own black vapour while retreating out of the flooded lake area altogether.'

'I think the pestilence and blight had begun to kick in by this time,' added Mike. 'The Fens had an organised and trusted form of defence. The Wake Men were becoming experienced in battling the fighting machines. I also think the Martians had bigger problems than our Fenlands.'

'Yeah, don't give us too much credit will you, Mike,' Corporal Parker replied sarcastically but with a hint of good humour. 'In short, I don't think we were of too much importance by this time.'

Kenworthy laughed. His beaming face shifted his grey moustache and neatly trimmed beard. 'I'm sure the Martians knew they were a little out of their league when they tried to take on the formidable Wake Men!'

'Hear, hear,' called a well-spoken voice.

Kenworthy stepped back and looked to Percival as the captain approached the small group of onlookers.

Sergeant Wickham and Corporal Parker stood to attention as the captain called, 'At ease, chaps, at ease.'

'Captain Paige,' said Wickham formally. 'May I present two reporters, Mr Humphrey Kenworthy and Mr Rupert Percival.'

'Glad to meet you, Mr Kenworthy.' Captain Paige bent forward and firmly shook the reporter's hand before doing likewise with the other man and saying, 'Pleased to meet you, Mr Percival.'

Percival was full of gratitude. 'Thank you, Captain. I presume you were formally Lieutenant Paige of the *Hereward* fighting crew. Your good fellows have been telling us this story. Dashed sad to know about Dr Cheema and Miss Clairmont. I'm presuming they were very fine people, Sir.'

'Very fine people indeed, Mr Percival.' Paige regarded the four men from the observation post with a look of sorrow, before continuing respectfully. 'I've been to the large tent, where the skeletons of the Wake Men Militia have been placed. Good people we lost in that final battle. All findings have been placed there. Lines of tables and each containing the remains of our fallen men – plus one young lady, who we believe to be Miss Clairmont. Dr Cheema is identified among the Wake too. Also, our illustrious loud corporal. Do you remember him?'

There followed a smattering of mixed feelings. All knew the demise of the brave people who took the fight to the invading Martians that night.

Wickham responded, 'The *Hereward* and the Wake Men met the challenge and prevailed.'

'Miss Clairmont was a fine lady. Dr Cheema was proud of her knowledge and support over those moments of discovery,' said Mike.

Parker sighed. 'Indeed, Dr Cheema was proud of Miss Clairmont. We lost so many good people. Every survivor from one end of the country to the other knows the heartache of lost ones. No person has escaped the anguish.'

'I can still hear that old corporal screaming out his defiant orders,' added Wickham, smiling sadly.

Then as though on request, Captain Paige grinned and asked, 'What was his famous call?'

The four men of the observation post replied in perfect time, 'WAKE MEN! WAKE MEN – ADVANCE!'